ACKNOWLEDGMENTS

My heartfelt thanks to my wonderful husband, Peter, for unwavering love and support.

My parents, James and Yvonne, and my granny Sara for always believing in me.

The editors at Genesis Press for giving me the creative freedom to break a BIG romance genre rule in this book with my hero, Jackson DeWitt. My muse hopes the gamble will pay off.

An extra special thanks to Genesis line editor Sidney Rickman, who always manages to keep me from embarrassing myself too much.

The readers who took the time to track me down and let me know they enjoyed my previous Indigo romances: *Picture Perfect* and *Yesterday's Dreams, Tomorrow's Promises*. I appreciate the feedback. Please visit my web site at reonlaudat.com.

IT'S IN HIS KISS

REON LAUDAT

Genesis Press, Inc.

Indigo

An imprint of Genesis Press, Inc.
Publishing Company

Genesis Press, Inc.
P.O. Box 101
Columbus, MS 39703

ISBN-13: 978-1-58571-348-6
ISBN-10: 1-58571-348-1
Manufactured in the United States of America

First Edition 2002
Second Edition 2009

Visit us at www.genesis-press.com or call at 1-888-Indigo-1

CHAPTER 1

No one ever said the restaurant business would be easy, Savannah Jacobs reminded herself as she stepped inside the back door of the Silver Spoon Cafe, the realization of her lifelong dream. But she hadn't counted on having her resolve tested relentlessly in one seventy-two-hour disaster-thon.

All hell had broken loose at her restaurant at noon last Friday, starting with the pipe that sprang a leak in the basement, soaking a year's supply of napkins and toilet paper.

Then there were the cockroaches, an army of them practically line dancing inside the bargain bags of flour.

She'd vowed never ever to purchase five-finger discount goods from a petty street hustler who answered to the nickname "Stank" again.

Murphy's Law had kicked in full throttle when Felix, her temperamental head cook, up and quit without the courtesy of a two-week notice. Just when she thought things couldn't get worse, some pervert flashed and scared away the last of her steadfast regulars the following Saturday.

Carrying a big basket of fresh sunflowers she would separate into table centerpieces, Savannah made her way to the kitchen where she deactivated the security system with a few quick jabs on a wall-mounted keypad.

Thank goodness for Mondays!

The start of a new week, filled with promise and yet another opportunity to make her six-month-old business the success she'd always envisioned.

First on her to-do list: Place a classified ad for a new head cook. Percy and Emma Jean were adequate assistant cooks at best, and only when supervised. They were going to need all the help they could get in the kitchen.

Savannah dropped her basket of sunflowers on a table and walked through the Silver Spoon flipping on the lights, central air and music system, as her heart filled with pride. The brick storefront restaurant boasted a decor that was a frisky, funky mingling of the contemporary and traditional. Recessed lights dotted a spectacular domed ceiling and warmed the pale gray and yellow walls. Matching damask cloth accented the circular tables. The muted colors under-scored the beauty of the aged, ebonized oak floor. A light blue glass-tiled wall separated the dining room from the kitchen. She'd splurged on the gilded mirrors adorning three of the walls and the Victorian upright piano, which held court in one corner. But if she had it all to do over again, she wouldn't change a thing. The Silver Spoon looked exactly as she'd envisioned it all those years ago when it was still just a silly dream. A smile curled her lips. All the hassles she'd endured in the six months since the restaurant opened were a small price to pay in exchange for the smiles and compliments from satisfied customers.

In the kitchen she flicked on the coffee maker and grabbed a banana nut muffin from one of the walk-in pantries. In the main dining room, she opened the blinds.

Her younger brother Troy emerged from the rear entrance. Relaxed khaki slacks and a crisp oxford shirt draped loosely over his thick, bullet-like build.

"Hey, kiddo," Savannah called out cheerily as she took a seat at a front table to enjoy her muffin and the warmth of the early morning sunshine. "Rough night?" she asked, noting the deep trench between his brows and the grim set of his lips.

Troy had turned twenty-six on his last birthday, but the three years she had on him meant her fretting and fussing would never end. A part of her would always regard him as her rascally little brother.

When their parents died in a tragic car accident, Troy had been ten and Savannah thirteen. Though shuttled through the foster care system, they'd miraculously been blessed with a caseworker who had worked diligently to keep them together. In addition to striving to be the world's greatest big sister, Savannah had assumed the role of protector, mother, father, and best friend. She'd recently added employer to that list when she hired Troy to help manage the Silver Spoon.

"I'm fine, sis. I was actually worried about you."
He leaned over to give her a peck on the cheek, before
claiming the chair beside hers. Through his trendy
wire-rimmed glasses, he gave her an appraising look.

"Me?" Savannah nibbled her muffin. "Oh, you
mean have I recovered from all this weekend's drama
with the pipes, the cockroaches, the flasher and Felix's
last-minute resignation? I'm happy to say I survived.
From now on it's only onward and upward for the
Silver Spoon." She released a wry chuckle. "What else
could possibly go wrong?"

Troy averted his gaze, then moved to the front of
the restaurant. He opened the door and grabbed the
newspaper and some department store sales circulars
on the ground just outside the threshold before
heading toward the kitchen.

Savannah went to him. "Hey, wait a minute. Isn't
that this morning's *Cincinnati Tribune*?" She reached
for it. "May I?"

"Are there any more of those muffins left?" Troy
asked, deftly moving the paper out of her grasp.

"Yeah, at least a dozen, in the left pantry. The
paper, please."

Troy blatantly ignored her outstretched hand.
"What about coffee? Did you make a pot?"

Savannah released a rueful sigh. "Yes, I made
coffee. Be right back." She disappeared through the
swinging doors leading to the kitchen, then returned
a few minutes later with two steaming cups of coffee.

"Two sugar cubes for you. And nondairy creamer with one sugar cube for me."

Troy reached for his cup and took a long sip. "So are you going to go through the applications on file to find a replacement for Felix or are you going to go for a fresh crop with a classified ad?"

Savannah sat and shrugged. "I think I'll do both. I need somebody quickly so I'll go through the filed applications today. I can't imagine that the *Tribune* can get my ad in until the day after tomorrow. Speaking of which, where is it? Hand it over."

"What?"

"The *Tribune,* silly!"

Troy paused and scrunched his face. With a sigh he got up and moved to the small trash can near the swinging door that led to the kitchen.

Savannah tried plucking the paper out of his hand. Troy snatched it back again.

"Troy!" Startled, Savannah reclaimed the paper. "What the hell is with you and the *Tribune* this morning?"

"I just thought after everything you went through this weekend…" His words trailed off.

"What?"

"Today's *Tribune* is the last thing you should see."

"Why? Did my Com-Tram stock take a nosedive? Does my horoscope say I'm going to get plowed over by a city bus?" Savannah chuckled as she quickly flipped through the metro, business and sports sections in search of her favorite part of the paper, a tabloid insert dubbed Out & About, which featured movies, plays and restaurant reviews. Unlike most newspapers, which usually published such entertainment and leisure sections on the weekends, the *Tribune* had tried a novel approach by releasing an extra one on Mondays, to give its readers a few days to plan ahead for their weekend outings. The experiment had proven to be a success. The section's debut had been credited with a huge jump in the paper's Monday circulation figures according to a story she'd read.

"I suppose you're going to find out sooner or later," Troy said quietly.

"Find out what?" Savannah asked as she sat and placed the Out & About section on top of a table in front of her. "Oh my gosh, Troy, look! Is this what you were talking about?" Her eyes went wide as she noisily rifled through the pages of the thick tab. "Looks as if they reviewed the Silver Spoon!" A smile swept across her face and her heart hammered wildly in her chest. "Do you know what this means? This could make us! The crowds will come clamoring and maybe we'll be operating in the black way ahead of schedule! This is so…so…" Her eyes skimmed the black and white pages. "Awful!"

She read the screaming headline out loud, "Gag Me with a Spoon?" Then, like a stiletto's stab to the heart, she saw the measly one-and-a-half star rating the reviewer had given her restaurant.

A jumble of emotions whirled inside of her—anger, hurt, humiliation—but she kept reading. She was like a gaping motorist passing a devastating car crash with mangled bodies. She could not look away.

A severed limb here: "The so-called Caesar salad was like a plate of tasteless iceberg lettuce drizzled with liquefied low-fat mayo."

A splatter of guts there: "The veal was tough and chewy. Old combat boot leather would have a more appetizing texture and consistency."

A disembodied head hurtling through the air: "Fettuccini alfredo should be called fettuccini, I'm afraid so. Or more accurately, bland buttery noodles in a flat, flavorless broth."

She read on as the carnage continued. Her lips trembled with despair as she saw her dreams of restaurant success slashed to death with the swift, vicious strokes of the reviewer's poison pen.

She slumped in her chair, crushing the paper against her chest.

"I'm sorry, Savannah." Troy placed his hand on top of hers in a consoling gesture. "I knew that review was going to break your heart. I wasn't sure whether to tell you about it right away or not—especially after the weekend we've had here. Business wasn't so good to begin with. When things finally started to pick up, all hell broke loose, and now this."

"My restaurant's not that bad, is it?" Savannah asked in a thin voice she didn't recognize as she reached for a napkin in a holder and dabbed at her teary eyes.

"No way! What does this…this… What's his name?" Troy pried the crumpled paper out of Savannah's grip and glanced at the byline above the Silver Spoon's scathing review. "What does this Jackson DeWitt know, anyway? Probably just had a bug up his butt that day he came in here and decided to take it out on the Silver Spoon."

"You think so?" Savannah sniffled, trying to grasp the optimism lifeline Troy hurled at her. "He shouldn't let his mood determine whether he will or won't trash people's dreams and destroy their livelihoods. Okay, so he didn't like the fettuccini, did he have to be so damn mean about it?"

"You know how those reviewers are," Troy replied. "A bad review is probably more fun to write. They can be so cute and witty, trotting out all their favorite wisecracks and put-downs. Besides, haven't you heard? Those who can do and those who can't review?"

Savannah's sadness gave way to anger. Her posture went rigid. "Well, I'm not going to let Mr. DeWitt get away with this."

"C'mon, Savannah, calm down."

"No, I'm not going to take this attack lying down." She checked her watch, where both hands met at nine. She had plenty of time to get to the *Tribune,* take care of her business with this Jackson DeWitt person, then make it back before the Silver Spoon was scheduled to open.

"Uh-uh, Savannah, I know that look in your eyes. I think I'd better tag along…"

She surged to her feet. "I'll be fine."

"I know you will. It's this Jackson DeWitt dude I'm worried about. He won't know what hit him."

❧

Jackson DeWitt sat at his desk at the *Cincinnati Tribune,* perusing a stack of crisp new menus and pondering his next reviews for upcoming months. What will it be? French, Korean, Ethiopian, Chinese, Thai, Italian, Classic American? And what combination?

"Hey Jackson." Angelica Alexander, the *Tribune* fashion editor, slinked over to his desk in a Tabasco-red business suit as spicy as the provocative swing in her hips. A former high fashion model turned fashion journalist, Angelica had legs for miles and seized every opportunity to show them off with itsy-bitsy skirts that barely grazed newsroom standards.

"My vote is for seafood," Angelica said with a saucy smile and a flirtatious wink. "You know what they say about oysters."

"Yeah, I know what they say about oysters, Angelica," Jackson replied with an indulgent smile as he tilted the back of his swivel chair.

Angelica had been trying to reel Jackson in with her power flirting since he'd begun working for the *Tribune* a year ago. He liked Angelica so he played along, but he never considered going beyond flirty repartee. As attractive as Angelica was, with her Playboy centerfold bosom and Vogue face, Jackson didn't believe a romantic dalliance was worth it. Dating a colleague would be asking for big workplace hassles.

"So what do you say?" Angelica asked, gazing at Jackson as if he were the most decadent treat on the dessert tray. "You could review that new seafood restaurant on the waterfront. What was the name of it? Cesaro's. Yeah, you can review Cesaro's and take me with you as a second taster."

"As tempting as that sounds, Angelica, my next restaurant is going to be this little Italian place on Sixth and I've already told Jim Butler and two other guys from sports that they could join me."

Angelica pouted and crossed her arms over voluptuous breasts that appeared too round, firm and upright to be natural. Gravity alone would not be so kind.

"I'm liable to get my feelings hurt if you don't ask me to join you soon. You've taken half the *Tribune* staff with you at some point or another."

Jackson shrugged. "What can I say? Everybody loves free food. The *Tribune* picks up the tab for my guests during these…um…culinary investigations, you know. That makes me a very popular guy around here."

"But I haven't had my invite yet. If I didn't know better, I'd think you didn't want to share a meal with me."

"The next time I do a seafood restaurant, I promise to invite you and Abigail. She loves seafood, too."

"Me and Abigail?" Angelica made a sour face. "Why do I have to share you with her?"

"Because she'll be retiring soon and she's a nice lady. I think we'd both enjoy her company," Jackson replied with tact, leaving off the most important part. Abigail's presence would insure the dinner would not be mistaken for anything other than what it was. A working evening out with two colleagues. "So is it a deal?"

Before Angelica could reply, a commotion broke out near the receptionist's desk. An attractive young cinnamon-skinned woman had entered the newsroom speaking loudly enough to trump the usual newsroom noise, which included blaring police scanners, ringing phones, tapping printers, several TV sets suspended from the ceiling and chatter.

He guessed her to be a tad shy of five feet four inches, but her short frame packed the kind of precipitous curves he loved. Her hair was cropped in one of those trendy spiky hairdos that showed off full bow lips, a pert nose and storied cheekbones. Absolutely stunning, Jackson thought, leveling the tilt of his swivel chair and resting the stack of files and restaurant menus on his desk. Abigail pointed in Jackson's direction and the beauty shot his way with the older woman on her heels, haplessly trying to impede her progress.

"Wait! Wait!" Abigail bellowed. "You can't just go storming over there if he's not expecting you."

Undeterred, the younger woman charged toward Jackson and, for the first time, he noticed she was carrying what looked like one of those Corningware dish thingies.

"You're Jackson DeWitt?" The muscle in her clenched jaw pulsed. Fire danced in her pretty brown eyes.

A winded Abigail clutched her chest. "I'm sorry, Jackson. She just took off before I could stop her. Should I phone security?"

Jackson glanced at Angelica. Curiosity lit his colleague's face as she quietly took in the drama.

Thoroughly intrigued, Jackson stood to his full six feet, three inches, thinking the twelve or so inches he had on this angry gatecrasher might be intimidating. She didn't flinch, but merely lifted her chin with the same defiant glare.

Despite his better judgment, he felt his lips kick up in a small smile. "That's all right, Abigail," Jackson answered when he gave the woman a quick head-to-toe perusal. Save for the serving dish in her hands, she didn't appear to be armed. And besides, he knew he could subdue this little curvaceous bundle of glowering heat if she became too disruptive. An image of himself sweeping her into his arms flashed through his mind while a hot wave of awareness rolled through his body.

Something he hadn't felt in seven long months. Something he wasn't even sure if or when he'd feel again.

"Yes, I'm Jackson DeWitt. And you are?" he asked.

"The owner of the Gag-Me-With-a-Spoon establishment you flamed in today's Out & About section," she ground out.

"Excuse me?" Jackson drew a blank.

"The Silver Spoon! The place that serves food you described as 'pedestrian at best!'" she clarified.

"The Silver Spoon? Oh, yeah," Jackson said with a nod. Then his hand went up to absently rub his clean-shaven chin. He had written that review last month, which in the newspaper business seemed like eons ago. He'd easily reviewed about a dozen restaurants since. Jackson usually tried to work with a four- to five-week lead-time and he hadn't had a chance to read that morning's newspaper, which was why he didn't connect the dots immediately.

"You said the consistency was way off and there wasn't enough heavy cream used in my…what did you call it? My Fettuccini-I'm-Afraid-So sauce, so we whipped up a special batch just for you." With that, she upended the serving dish. A glob of greasy noodles landed on his stack of menus with a splat.

"What the hell…?" Jackson yelled, hands flying up. "You're nuts!"

The woman then proceeded to whip out a piece of newsprint he suspected was his review. She shredded it into little pieces and sprinkled them on top. "A new garnish I'm experimenting with! Enjoy!"

She plunked the serving dish down beside the glob of noodles, then with a dramatic pivot she stalked away.

"Hey, you, wait a minute!" Jackson called after her, but she didn't spare him a second glance as she exited the newsroom and darted to the bank of elevators in the hallway. Jackson went after her. "Hey, you, come back here right this minute and clean up this mess!" As she disappeared behind the sealed elevator doors, he stopped short, blinking in utter disbelief. He could've sworn she'd poked her tongue out at him, then given him the finger!

He loped back to his desk. For the first time since that little spitfire appeared, he noticed that all eyes in the newsroom were on him. Angelica snapped out her own stupor. "They really oughta tighten the security around this place. That was downright scary. What if she were packing something besides pasta?"

Jackson dropped in his seat as the scent of hot Parmesan cheese rushed up his nose.

"Hey, Jackson!" one of the guys from the pool of sports reporters called out. "What a hot dish! And I'm not talking about that goop she dumped on your desk, either!"

A real hot-tempered dish. That she certainly was. Jackson wasn't so startled he hadn't noticed that she was indeed a stunner. She was a little neurotic, with a definite flare for the dramatic to boot. But he wasn't going to rest until he got a full name from the mystery woman who'd managed to ruin his pristine stack of restaurant files, insult him with an obscene gesture and ignite a flicker of a fire inside of him—all in a few short minutes.

CHAPTER 2

Savannah felt a lot better after evening the score with that awful dream crusher Jackson DeWitt. She returned to the restaurant determined to carry on business as usual. After wrapping up a half-hour interview with the first job applicant on her list, she prepared to escort the woman to the door and phone the next candidate.

"So when do you think you'll decide who gets the job?" The woman appeared to be at least ten years older than the twenty-six years she'd indicated on her application. Lank brown hair stretched to frizzy split ends, which straddled bony shoulders. Her slight frame was lost inside the faded thrift store dress.

Savannah didn't want to dismiss the woman with false hope, but she tended to have a hard time doling out rejection. "Well, Ms. Johnson," Savannah began, reaching for her pile of applications.

"Please call me Clara," the young woman corrected her.

Deciding the woman deserved the truth, Savannah released a heavy sigh. "Well, Clara, you really don't have the type of experience I'm looking for." She glanced at Clara's application again. "When you wrote that you'd worked in the kitchen at Emilio's for five years, I assumed you meant in some cook or chef capacity. I'm really not looking for a dishwasher or another bus person at this time."

"But I need a job so badly." The woman's voice quavered and her gray eyes turned glassy with unshed tears.

"I wish I could help, but…"

"See, when little Michael got sick, it threw our whole world into turmoil. The medical bills alone will make it almost impossible for my family to get back on our feet financially. My husband already works three jobs. And I have a night job cleaning offices, but I've always needed something at a restaurant…"

"Why a restaurant?" Savannah asked, conceding that she'd been drawn into the woman's sad tale.

"It's…it's the leftovers, you see," she said with downcast eyes.

"You take leftovers home to your family?" Savannah asked as her heart squeezed.

Clara's head came up. "Don't get me wrong. I've never stolen from any of the restaurants I've worked for, but I figure stuff that's going in the trash anyway…well…it's not hurting anybody."

Savannah knew it didn't make good business sense, but she simply couldn't turn the woman away. "Look, Clara, again, I don't need a dishwasher or bus person, but…"

"Yes?" Clara prompted as her voice hitched with hope.

"I…well…I could probably use another waitress, but I'm afraid I can only pay you to work part time."

"Bless you. Bless you." The woman came to her feet and reached for Savannah's hands to squeeze. Her weary gray eyes gleamed with new light. "You won't regret this decision. I'll work very hard for you."

"But I do have one rule," Savannah added. "No taking customer table scraps home to your family." The joy on Clara's pale face was about to drain completely away when Savannah added, "No scraps and picked over cast-offs, I mean. You have a family of four—you, your husband, son, mother-in-law, right? Well, you will be allowed to take one plate of whatever the day's Silver Spoon special is for each member of your family as part of your benefits package. Is that a deal?"

The smile returned to Clara's face as she nodded enthusiastically. "Yes, ma'am. Thank you so much. I could tell when I first met you, you had a kind and generous spirit, Ms. Jacobs."

"You can start tomorrow morning." Savannah walked Clara through the kitchen to the back door. "And one more thing."

"Yes, anything Ms. Jacobs." Clara beamed as she stepped over the threshold.

"Please stop calling me Ms. Jacobs," Savannah scolded the woman playfully. "Savannah will do just fine."

"Okay, Savannah."

Savannah closed the door, still one head chef short and one part-time waitress over-staffed. She should probably toughen up, but she'd found it way more difficult to harden her heart against other people's misfortune when she could just as easily extend a hand to help. Her ex-husband, Bryce, had always chastised Savannah for that very tendency.

He'd made a killing with some patented computer chip device he parlayed into millions. But he'd been so tight with a buck he refused to "splurge" on toilet paper that didn't feel like dried oak leaves. Bryce had claimed Savannah was a real patsy for every crook, creep and lowlife with a sob story. He'd been right about her weakness for creeps. Bryce had turned out to be the biggest one of all. After swapping I do's, Savannah's knight in shining armor morphed into a rusted tin man with a big clump of blue chip stock where his heart had once been.

Once he'd struck it rich, all he cared about was making more money. And appearances. Being seen with the right snots and snobs at the right hoity-toity social functions. Soon Savannah had outgrown him, emotionally and literally. She simply would not act the part of the lunching-high-society lady who lifted a manicured pinkie only for the most prestigious chari-table boards. But when her figure expanded beyond the size two Barbie clothes she'd worn for so many years, Bryce no longer attempted to hide his mounting disgust. He stopped making love to her as punishment. Then he'd hurled insult after insult, claiming it was his version of tough love, a wake-up call to motivate her to get her act together. She'd been put on notice. Shape up or ship out. His ultimatum, among other grievances, had only prompted Savannah to reach for more jelly donuts and the Yellow Pages to track down a good divorce attorney.

With part of her divorce settlement she'd purchased the Silver Spoon. Bryce's ego had been throttled when Savannah dumped him first. How dare this "lumpy-bumpy" woman walk out on him, he'd declared as he watched the last of Savannah's belongings get loaded onto the moving truck that pulled up to the gorgeous eight-bedroom mansion they'd once shared. When Bryce got wind of her restaurant plan, he'd exploded, then predicted the establishment's imminent demise.

"What's a scatterbrain like you doing trying to run a business?" Bryce had said, his tone thick with malicious intent. "I'll give you one year, just one year, before it flops."

Savannah cringed at the thought of Bryce seeing that *Tribune* restaurant review. She tried to take consolation in the fact that it was already close to five p.m. and she hadn't heard from him yet. If he had seen the review, no doubt he wouldn't bypass an opportunity to rub it in. Maybe he was out of town on a business trip and would miss perusing the newspaper. She supposed she shouldn't care what Bryce thought. She sure as hell wasn't going to let some bozo like Jackson DeWitt and his poison pen take her down.

As miffed as she was by that restaurant critic, she couldn't help recalling his smoldering good looks. He'd cut a striking figure as he chased her to the elevator. Her anger might have rendered her inconsolable at the time, but not blind. The man was supa dupa fine!

His long muscle-molded frame was sheer perfection to behold. And that face looked as if it had been chiseled by an artist using her steamiest dreams for inspiration. Thick silken brows slashed above dark eyes that held the best kind of secrets. Savannah felt her insides go aflutter just thinking about him. But it was best to sweep the studly jerk to the back of her mind. All she had to do was peek out at the empty dining room to rekindle her resolve.

Troy swept through the swinging door separating the dining area from the kitchen. "So how was that applicant who just left? Do we have ourselves a new cook?"

Savannah gave him a sheepish smile. "No, but we have ourselves a new part-time waitress."

"Sa-van-nah," Troy drew out the syllables of her name as always when he was irritated with her. "You know we don't need and can't afford to add to the serving staff right now. We need a head cook or chef. Pronto."

"I know." Savannah wrung her hands. "But—"

Troy cut her off. "Okay, but out of curiosity, what was the story this time? The roof caved in, crippling the dog and flat-lining the cat? Granny needs a new pair of orthopedic shoes?"

"Oh, Troy, am I that transparent?"

"Yes," he said, drawing her in for a quick hug. "I know you just can't help yourself. You have a big heart. It's one of your strengths and sometimes your biggest weakness."

"But she and her family were living off table scraps at Emilio's," Savannah said by way of an explanation.

"She worked at Emilio's? Did you happen to phone them to find out why she's not employed there anymore?"

Savannah realized her impulsive hiring decision had made even less business sense. She should've done the obligatory follow-up, checking references before promising the woman a job, but she'd gone with her gut feeling that Clara would be a hard-working, trust-worthy employee. "No, I didn't, but trust me on this one. I think she'll work out fine. And about the head cook job, I'm going to line up at least three more applicants for tomorrow. We'll have that position filled in no time."

Daphne, one of the three servers waiting out a dead dinner shift, interrupted them. "Savannah, there's a customer out there, a very handsome customer, I might add, asking to see the owner."

"Remember the customer is always right, give him whatever he wants," Savannah said, with a dismissive flap of her hand. "Even if he screwed up his order, it's our fault, okay?"

"He hasn't ordered yet, but you'd better believe that brother will get service with a smile." Daphne winked.

Propelled by curiosity, Savannah moved to the door and pushed it just enough to peek through. She jumped away, plastering herself against an adjacent wall. "It's him!" she shrieked.

"Him who?" Troy went to the door and peeked out.

"Him! You know, the jerk who ripped the Silver Spoon in today's Out & About section in the *Tribune*."

Emma Jean, who was starting her shift as a cook, had just entered the kitchen through the back door. She tugged on her rubber food preparation gloves. "Want me to put rat poison in his rotelli?"

"He hasn't ordered rotelli or anything else yet," Daphne told Emma Jean. "He just wants to see our boss lady. Well?"

"Well what?" Savannah asked stupidly.

"Aren't you going to see what he wants?" Daphne gave Savannah a befuddled look.

"I'll take care this." Troy headed for the door.

Savannah blocked his path. "No! Wait! I'll fight my own battles." She squared her shoulders and clenched her jaw just before pushing through the swinging door. She crossed her damn near empty dining room. On the left side sat an old white-haired gentleman named Mr. Watowski, who'd come in almost every week since The Silver Spoon opened. He'd nurse one tall glass of sweetened ice tea and a bowl of their soup of the day. Monday meant he was hunched over a serving of chicken and barley. As usual Savannah made her way to his table to give him a warm smile and inquire whether that day he'd venture to try something different from the menu.

The scene always played out the same. He'd tease and say he'd take one Savannah wrapped up in a red ribbon to go.

Then Savannah would say, "But I'm not on the menu, Mr. Watowski."

Then he'd say, "Well, you oughta be listed under the desserts because you're as sweet as pie."

Corny, but the old man's kind words had never failed to make Savannah smile. After spending much of the day reeling from the fallout of that bad review, she drew strength from their routine.

Savannah left Mr. Watowski and approached Jackson DeWitt's table. "I'm told you wanted to see me," she said in a crisp voice.

"Oh, don't go all stiff and formal on me now, Savannah." His baritone glided over the syllables of her name like silk.

"How do you know my name?"

"Daphne told me. Cute girl." He grinned, sending her pulse racing. "She wasn't my server that night I came in to review the place. I would've remembered meeting her."

Savannah felt a twinge of jealousy, but wasn't sure why. All she knew about this man was that he'd displayed a ruthless disregard for struggling restaurateurs such as herself.

"I'm not sure why you're here unless you're a glutton for punishment," Savannah said facetiously. "I mean, why would a man with your superior, discriminating taste buds subject himself to more...," she made quote marks with her fingers, "'pedestrian cuisine?'"

Jackson reached for the brown paper bag that she'd just noticed on the table. "I came to return this."

"What is it?" Savannah scrutinized the bag in his outstretched hand, but wouldn't accept it.

"Don't worry. It's not ticking," he said, as the sexy grin settled on his handsome face again. "It's the serving dish you left after you dumped your other hot, goopy calling card on my desk."

"If you're here for an apology, you're not going to get one." Savannah affected her best haughty look, nose in the air and pinched lips.

"Duly noted. You may unclench now." Jackson gestured toward the chair across from his. "Please, have a seat. You're making me nervous, hovering over me like Mrs. Weddle in fifth period study hall."

"Mrs. Weddle?"

"Never mind." He chuckled at what was obviously some inside joke.

Savannah literally stood her ground. "If you're not going to order something you're going to have to move it along, buster. We don't encourage loiterers."

Jackson made quite a show of scanning his surroundings. The dining room was so desolate, Savannah half expected a couple of tumbleweeds to roll by.

"I can see the joint is really jumping tonight," he said drolly.

"Thanks to you and that scathing review!" Savannah felt her blood go from a slow simmer to a raging boil. "Now, if you're going to order something, fine. I'll send cute Daphne out to take care of it. If not, I'd appreciate it if you'd leave."

"Excuse me?"

"You heard me. Make like a banana split. Or make like the wind and break."

Up shot his brows.

"Um, I mean, make like the wind and blow," she flushed and added quickly.

"What if I say I'm not ready to leave yet?" he asked in an unflappable way that grated.

If she'd had another bowl of fettuccini alfredo in her hands right then, she'd dump it on his head. "I can't believe you have the nerve to show your face here after what you've done." Unleashing a day's worth of frustration, she wagged her finger so close to his nose he went cross-eyed. "Have you ever thought of all the lives you could ruin if this place goes under? Huh? No, I think not! You sit behind your little desk, pecking away on your little keyboard, wreaking havoc on beleaguered new entrepreneurs when the whim hits you!"

That composed facade of his finally cracked and the muscle in his jaw flexed. "When the whim hits me? I have a job to do, lady. And I'd like to think I'm very good at it. I know food and I'm fair. I do not dole out bad reviews on a whim. And I always visit restaurants at least twice to make sure I'm not just catching a place on one off night. I made two trips to the Silver Spoon and both times I found it woefully lacking. Oh sure, you have a nice setup here with the decor and all, but the fancy antique piano and flattering lighting won't do squat to satisfy a diner's raging hunger pangs. And you want to talk about fair? Just how fair is it to expect people to pay their hard-earned cash for inferior food and service, especially at these prices you're charging. They're ridiculous." He lifted the menu off the table and waved it at her before slapping it back down. "Do you have any idea what you're doing here? The restaurant business is hard and it ain't for the weak. One out of every three restaurants in the U.S. is doomed for failure in its first two years of operation. You'd better get your act together, lady, before you become another statistic."

Narrowing her eyes, Savannah practically vibrated with fury. "Get out. Get of my restaurant right now," she whispered with queasy menace.

A silence fell between them and a scorching staredown ensued.

Jackson visibly surrendered, then issued a speedy mea culpa. "Look, I'm sorry. I don't get off being cruel." His tone softened and he ran his fingers through his short curls. "I'm trying to be straight with you. Hey, I know a bad review is like taking a punch to the gut, but it's not too late to correct your mistakes. I know of restaurants that have survived temporary shutdown orders from the health department. Surely it would take more than one bad newspaper review to sink you."

"You've already noted that business isn't exactly banging." Savannah reluctantly sat in one of the chairs at his table. "We were just working out some of the kinks and experiencing a minor upswing in business the last four weeks, when the pipes in the basement burst Friday, my head cook quit and a pervert who couldn't keep his whacker in his pants came calling. Then your review."

"You had a flasher?" Jackson's brow pleated with concern.

"Yeah, and he wasn't good for business either," Savannah replied dryly. "Had to call the cops to make sure he wasn't still lurking about outside somewhere. A couple of female patrons that night were afraid to leave, fearing the weirdo might follow them home. Think those two will ever come back or encourage their family and friends to come here? I seriously doubt it."

"Sorry about that."

"You mean sorry it didn't happen on your watch, when you were here working your review black magic." Savannah couldn't keep the edge out of her tone. "I'm sure that would have made a tasty little morsel for your column. You could've had a field day with all the bad weenie puns."

"I don't do hot dog puns, period. Too juvenile," he replied.

"Like a headline such as 'Gag Me With Spoon' is so sophisticated? Not only was it dumb, but dated, downright prehistoric." Savannah launched into her own exaggerated litany of ancient eighties teen speak. "I mean really, that's so like bitchin', man, omigosh, like so grodie to the max and totally, totally valley girl."

Jackson chuckled in earnest and for the first time since Savannah approached his table she did, too.

"I like your laugh," Jackson said, eroding the wall of anger between them so quickly it rattled her. "And for the record, I don't write the headlines. That's a copy editor's job."

After everything, she did not want to be charmed by this man in particular. But there she was, sneaking peeks at the gilded mirror on an adjacent wall. Suddenly she wondered if her breath was fresh and if specks of black ground pepper from the pastrami she'd had for dinner had wedged themselves in her smile. She ran her tongue over her front teeth, then discreetly raked her fingers through her cropped hairdo. His penetrating gaze caused her cheeks to flush.

After a pensive moment he leaned toward her. "I have a proposition for you, Savannah."

She lifted one brow. "Oh?"

"I'm willing to share what I know about food and the restaurant business—"

Savannah interrupted with an incredulous laugh. "There's certainly no dearth of confidence on your part, is there, Mr. DeWitt? You're so sure you have something to say that I need to hear?"

"Well, you'd be a fool not to take me up on this offer. I don't mean to boast, but maybe I oughta run down my credentials for you. In addition to having a degree in journalism from Missouri, one the top journalism schools, I managed to complete two years of food preparation study at The Culinary Institute of New Orleans and I've had extensive seminar training in restaurant management. I even took that food handlers certification course they offer at the health department."

"Oh," Savannah replied, trying not to sound impressed, though she most certainly was. "If you've got all that going for you, why aren't you actively participating in the business by running your own restaurant or catering service?"

"Isn't it obvious? I love writing about food and restaurants," Jackson replied. "But we're not talking about me right now. This is about you and the survival of the Silver Spoon. I'm offering the benefit of my knowledge."

"My budget won't allow for any hefty consultation fees, Mr. DeWitt." As Savannah leaned toward him, she noticed the almost imperceptible dip of Jackson's head when he ventured a quick glance at her breasts. She wondered if he liked what he saw, then she snapped erect, instantly mortified by her thoughts. Her brains were scrambling as her hormones mutinied.

"My fee would be your time."

"My time?" Savannah had to admit she was thoroughly intrigued. She checked his ring finger and found it bare. Was he going to ask her on a date? She didn't find the thought as unappealing as she should have under the circumstances. Did she dare say yes? Or should she tell him to take a flying leap? After all, this was the man she'd loathed, even more than tripe and boiled okra, just a few minutes ago. However, she found it next to impossible to hang onto righteous indignation when he looked at her with sexy brown eyes that made her want to break into an impromptu table dance. Get a grip, Savannah!

"Yes. I have a twelve-year-old niece, Sasha. She's something else, I'll tell you." Jackson's features went soft, as if he'd been seized by a pleasant thought. "Anyway, Sasha's Sunbeam Girl troop is always looking for guest speakers, usually career women with interesting occupations. Entrepreneurs such as yourself are usually big hits with the girls."

"So I'd be a good role model for these little girls even though you think my restaurant is a major flop?"

"You're not an official failure until you hang a going-out-of-business sign," Jackson said. "And you don't strike me as the type who would give up so easily."

Savannah's lips curled into a provocative smile. "And so you think you've already got me figured out?"

"Enough to safely venture that you just might be curious enough to take me up on my offer." Jackson pulled himself up to his full height of six-feet-plus.

The masculine aura surrounding him could melt polar ice caps. Savannah decided it was no use fighting her obvious knee-weakening attraction to him.

With long, elegant fingers, Jackson reached inside his fashionable sport jacket pocket and removed a slim, gold case which contained his business cards. He placed one on the table. "I'll be waiting for your call," he said just before he tucked the card case back into his pocket, then turned to exit the Silver Spoon.

Savannah waited a full five minutes before collapsing against the back of her chair with a breathy swoon. "Wow," she said, fanning herself with his card.

A couple of hours later, back in her office, Savannah and Troy pored over their receipts for the day, a painfully short task because business had been so lousy.

"Let me get this straight. You're making nice with the man who publicly flayed the Silver Spoon for all the world to read?" Troy had settled on the seat in front of Savannah's chaotic desk. Tall, untidy stacks of paper crowded most of its surface.

"'For all the world to read'? Don't you think that's a bit of an exaggeration?" Savannah asked as she keyed numbers into the spreadsheet on her computer screen.

"Don't you know the *Tribune* posts all its restaurant reviews on its Web site?"

Savannah swiveled her chair to face Troy. "What difference does it make now if someone in Botswana thinks our veal Parmesan sucks?"

"Whoa!" Troy nailed her with an incredulous look. "What's with the attitude adjustment? I mean, I'm glad you're not still stewing over that review, but this…this is a complete about-face. What did that DeWitt dude say to you, anyway?"

"To be honest, I got to thinking. If one lousy review could sink the Silver Spoon, that would mean it was a pretty pitiful restaurant to begin with. And you know me, I am a fighter. We will get beyond this. And I have to admit there is much room for improvement here. I'm still new at this and I have so much to learn. But the Silver Spoon will rebound and get better than ever," she said, pumped up with the adrenaline that came with a challenge. "Turns out Mr. DeWitt has these impressive food service credentials and he's willing to share his expertise with me. I guess it's his way of making up for the review."

"Wait a minute here." Behind his wire-rimmed specs Troy's eyes went wide. "And you're willing to take this guy up on his offer?"

"Why not? I hate to admit it, but we could definitely use his help. And he wouldn't get paid to evaluate restaurants for a respectable newspaper if he didn't know his stuff, right?"

"I suppose, but this morning you took off for the *Tribune* ready to ram Jackson DeWitt's poison pen down his pompous throat. This doesn't have anything to do with the fact that you haven't been on a real date in… What's it been?"

"One year, two months, one week and three days," Savannah chirped. "And the answer to your other question is, of course, my making nicey-nicey with Mr. DeWitt has something to do with that, too. Did you get a glimpse of that man?" Savannah lifted the restaurant's water bill off the desk and began fanning with it. "He's damn hot looking."

"So he's single?"

Savannah opened her mouth to reply, then faltered.

"Well?" Troy prodded.

"To tell the truth, I didn't ask. I checked out his ring finger and found it bare," she replied, then noted Troy's skeptical expression. "I know that doesn't mean anything, but it's a good sign. Besides, he's requested my presence—"

"For a date?"

"Not exactly," Savannah added with a sheepish smile. "It's more like my presence at his twelve-year-old niece's Sunbeam Girl troop meeting."

"How romantic," Troy replied with more than a tinge of sarcasm as he settled back in his chair. "I wonder what this dude is really up to. Something's not adding up."

"Why are you always so suspicious, Troy?"

"And you're not?" He sat upright and inched to the edge of his seat again. "As if you haven't been suspicious of my dates. Every woman I've gone out with in the past six months hasn't passed muster."

"That's only because I want the best for you." Savannah reached for his hands and squeezed. "I'd hate to see you make the same mistakes I did with Bryce."

"Speaking of Bryce, did you hear from him today?"

"No, and he obviously hasn't seen that review yet or he would've surely called to say 'I told you so.'"

"Jerk," Troy deadpanned. "Speaking of jerks, are you sure making a play for DeWitt is a smart move?"

"Absolutely," she replied, "I need to stop taking everything so seriously and have a little more fun. I haven't dated in over a year. And besides that, I've always hung back and waited to get chosen by someone. And I felt obliged to act grateful whenever someone did. It's as if somehow I never thought I was good enough to actually do the choosing. If there's one thing that joke of a marriage to Bryce taught me, it's that I'm responsible for my own happiness, which requires a more proactive approach."

"I, for one, am glad you're taking a more assertive approach, sis, but you still have to be careful who you take up with. I know you've been lonely——"

"And curling up with a big stack of steamy romance novels just ain't cuttin' it anymore—if you know what I mean. If anything they're making me crazier."

"Translation—hornier. Is that what we're talking about here?"

Savannah leveled her gaze at him. "And what if I am? Is that so wrong? I'm a grown woman with needs, Troy. I love spending time with you, little brother, but I know I've been cramping your style too much lately. It would be nice to spend some of my leisure time with someone who isn't related to or working for me. Know what I mean? Someone who could catch a movie, a concert, a play with me…"

"Among other things," Troy added with a bawdy mischief in his voice.

Savannah wadded a sheet of paper and lobbed it at his head. "Yes, among other things. And I've been dying to see that musical at the Aronoff Center ever since it came to town two weeks ago. You know, the one about the love affair between the Nubian slave and Egyptian prince. It sounds so romantic."

"*Aida*, right? What's stopping you?"

"It would be nice to see a show like that with a real date. You're a guy so you probably don't under-stand—"

"Just because I don't understand your addiction to those bodice-rippers of yours doesn't mean I don't know or care anything about romance."

"But as much as I love romance novels," Savannah corrected him, "why should I settle for a phantom paperback hero who only lives on the fringes of my fantasies? I say fringes because it's not as if there's a remote control to my subconscious that allows me to choose who shows up in my dreams and when. I'm lucky if the dashing, dapper romance-novel dude shows up at all. Most nights I have these bizarre dreams where I'm serving cheese fondue to Santa Claus, who is playing a rousing game of bid whist with Busta Rhymes and Anna Nicole Smith."

"And you think this Jackson DeWitt might be interested?"

"I don't know that for sure, but I'd like to find out," Savannah replied, primed to wax rhapsodic. "He certainly looks the part of the dashing hero, doesn't he? Tall, dark and hands-on handsome!" She rippled her fingers.

"I wouldn't know anything about that. But just be careful," Troy said thoughtfully, before coming to his feet. "I still say there's something about his showing up here that makes me uneasy. Speaking of which, about his offer to help you, isn't that some sort of conflict of interest?"

Savannah shook her head. "He's already panned the restaurant. His official newspaper business with the Silver Spoon is done. He won't be writing another review on us anytime soon—if ever. Any additional Silver Spoon reviews will have to be done by the *Tribune*'s competition, the Cincinnati *Examiner* or one of the local weeklies."

Troy made his way to the door. "I'm gonna lock up the back door. I'll swing back here on my way out so I can walk you to your car."

Savannah watched him leave, then removed Jackson's business card from her pocket. A smile teased her lips as she ran the pad of her index finger over its black embossed lettering. She sighed, recalling how his mocha skin stretched over long limbs thick with sculpted muscle. But before she allowed herself to get too caught up in her fantasies, she would have to verify two things. Was Jackson free to be pursued? And was he open to being pursued by her?

❧

Jackson returned to his house that night with Savannah on his mind. He thought he could still smell her soft, flirty fragrance—at once fresh as new rain and as zesty as salsa. Her appearance in the newsroom earlier that day had rocked his world in pleasantly surprising ways.

He hadn't really thought things through when he'd extended an offer to help with her restaurant. The place had potential: a stellar location, a great look, an owner who was willing to work to bring everything else up to par. There'd been a few items on the menu that were actually quite good. The desserts came to mind. But the mouth-watering cheesecake and apple pie had not been enough to outweigh what he'd deemed inferior. He sat on the side of his king-sized bed and removed his shoes. Still, he felt dishonest because he hadn't revealed the whole truth to Savannah as he'd planned.

It had been hard enough reasoning with her in an excitable state, but when she'd finally stopped lashing out at him he'd found it impossible to intentionally disappoint her. He'd been mesmerized by the sparkle in her eyes and the playful curve of her lips when she smiled. He'd known the woman less than twenty-four hours and she'd already impacted him significantly. He removed his clothes and quickly changed into pajama bottoms. He crawled between the covers and reached to turn off the lamp on the nightstand.

Sometime after closing his eyes, an image of Savannah appeared. She stood before him, naked and glistening like a goddess, beckoning him with outstretched hands. He saw himself go to her. He swept her off her feet and she wrapped her tawny legs around his hips. He enjoyed the feel of her lush breasts pressing against his chest. His fingers dallied at the silken trench of her back as she clung to him like a wild curling vine. His hands slid lower, sinking into the warm plush fullness of her bottom. The kind of bottom that refused to be ignored, no matter what she wore. Just the way he preferred them. He still didn't "get" the men who went for the stringy type, with puny butts that barely registered as a speed bump between their backs and legs.

As the seductive image grew more vivid, Savannah thrust her hips against him again and again. Jackson suddenly gasped in rapture, yanking himself out of the first sexual fantasy he'd had in months.

He awakened and bolted upright, groaning when he realized it was just a dream. Utter amazement, then relief washed over him as he reached for the lamp on the nightstand. Light flooded the room. He felt, then saw the full-fledged erection tenting his sheets. "Welcome back, old buddy. Wasn't sure when or if I'd see you again," he said as a smile settled on his face.

CHAPTER 3

The next day Jackson sat behind his desk at the *Tribune* and made several attempts to crank out the review for a new sushi bar he'd recently visited. His thoughts keep circling back to Savannah, and from there to that day four weeks ago when Larry Prescott had called him into his office to discuss Jackson's upcoming reviews.

At the time Jackson had thought it was odd that Prescott, the publisher and the highest-ranking executive at the *Tribune*, was taking such a personal interest in the restaurant column. The two had only spoken casually a few times when they'd shared elevator rides. And even then the conversation was limited to the innocuous "How about those Reds?" types of remarks. But that day when Jackson had been summoned to the plush office on the top floor of the 25-story building, it soon became apparent that Prescott really didn't give a damn about Jackson's column in general, but one particular review—the one he'd just completed on the Silver Spoon. After engaging in about twenty minutes of ice-breaking banter about the NBA championship games, Prescott had inquired about Jackson's impressions of the Silver

Spoon. As Jackson revealed that he'd panned the place, he'd taken note of Prescott's relieved expression. Though Jackson had tried to question the publisher about his odd reaction, Jackson had been ushered out of the office suite so quickly it was a wonder he hadn't gotten windburn in the process.

A colleague later revealed that according to newsroom scuttlebutt, a close friend of Prescott's was calling in a favor and pressuring the publisher to make sure the *Tribune* reviewed and—more importantly—slammed the Silver Spoon. That friend had been a local nouveaux riche entrepreneur named Bryce Martin, who'd launched a personal crusade to make sure his ex-wife's business venture ultimately failed.

Jackson had been livid when he recalled how he'd been manipulated into reviewing the Silver Spoon in the first place. The restaurant had not been on his initial review roster, but had come to him as a "top-priority assignment from someone in top management," he'd been told by his immediate supervisor. He'd received assignments like that before from his editor and hadn't thought twice about them. As long as top management wasn't dictating the content of his reviews, he hadn't been offended by such special requests.

But something about this one stank—that meeting in Prescott's office and the man's obvious relief when Jackson revealed that he indeed planned to rip the Silver Spoon. What if Jackson had penned a glowing review? Might he have been strong-armed into writing a less complimentary piece? That question bothered him.

Jackson also didn't like the idea of someone like Bryce Martin trying to use him and the *Tribune* to seek revenge on a woman, who was obviously trying to move on and carve out a new life for herself.

The night before Jackson had gone to the restaurant set on letting Savannah know what he thought her ex-husband was up to, but decided against it.

For one, Jackson didn't have any proof, just office gossip, to back up his suspicions.

And second, Jackson had written a less-than-stellar review of Savannah's restaurant. He'd written it in good conscience and given the Silver Spoon what he thought it had deserved at the time. That one-and-a-half star rating had absolutely nothing to do with him trying to appease his publisher.

But Savannah didn't know Jackson all that well and she sure as hell didn't trust him. Not yet anyway. So how was he going to convince her that he'd unwittingly done exactly what Prescott and Bryce Martin had wanted him to do?

But most importantly, he realized he couldn't tell her the truth just yet because he'd been enchanted by the woman. He refused to risk blowing the opportunity to get to know her better. He'd come clean later, but in the meantime, he'd do all he could to help Savannah polish the Silver Spoon. He reached for the phone on the desk and dialed directory assistance for the restaurant's number. Soon Savannah was on the line.

"Have you made a decision about my offer?" Jackson idly tapped an ink pen against his neatly arranged desk.

"So you were serious?" Savannah chuckled lightly.

"Of course I was. What do you say?"

"I say…"

When Savannah paused, Jackson realized he was actually holding his breath.

"I'll try you out, on a trial basis—"

"A trial basis? I thought I explained that there's no money or contracts involved."

"I know, but I'm just letting you know I might not be interested in a long-term commitment. We'll take it one meeting at a time. If I like what I hear, then we'll set up another meeting and so on—"

"Wait a second here. You're acting as if you're doing me a favor." Jackson kept his tone all business, but he felt his lips kicking up in a smile.

"I am, by still agreeing to have anything to do with you after the pummeling you gave my restaurant in print."

"So you're obviously not going to forgive me for simply doing my job?"

"Not just yet, anyway."

"Without some groveling."

"Oh, we can start with groveling," she parried.

"So you got some time to meet with me later on after work? I get off at seven."

Savannah paused, then replied, "I hate to be negative, but I doubt there will be a dinner rush here, so seven is fine."

"I look forward to seeing you again," Jackson said, before ending the call. He leaned back in his chair, cradling the back of his head in linked fingers.

"Well, hello, Jackson." Angelica appeared and shelved her rear on an edge of his desk. When her short skirt slipped up her thighs, he caught a glimpse of the garter belt attached to her stockings. "What do you think?" She crossed her long silky legs at the knee. "I'm doing a feature story on how stockings are making a big comeback."

"I didn't know they'd gone AWOL."

"True, they've always been around, but they'd been overshadowed by the convenience of pantyhose. But I've always thought stockings were much sexier."

"I see." Jackson pivoted his chair away from Angelica's gams to focus on his computer screen.

"So what do you think? Are you a pantyhose or stockings man?" She leaned toward Jackson, providing yet another panoramic view of her cleavage. "Or do you prefer bare legs? Or skin to skin?" she added with a heavily perfumed whisper.

Angelica's flirting had grown more brazen by the day. By office standards, she'd crossed over to what some might consider sexual harassment. But Jackson was more entertained than irritated by Angelica's antics. What single, red-blooded heterosexual guy would have a problem with a beautiful woman so eager to get his attention?

"So which do you prefer?" she prodded.

"It depends," Jackson replied as he began typing on his keyboard.

"On what?"

"On whom the legs are attached to. But I can say without a doubt control-top support hose like my Big Mama Etta used to wear probably won't do a thing for me."

Angelica threw her head back and laughed, flinging her long black mane over her shoulders and scattering the oriental notes of her expensive perfume.

"So when is our big seafood night?" she asked.

"I haven't checked with Abigail yet, but I'll get back to you on that," Jackson replied.

"So you're still set on inviting Abigail to be the third wheel?"

"Well, technically, Angelica, you'd be the third wheel since I promised Abigail she could join me for seafood first."

Angelica slid off his desk. As she prepared to sashay to her cubicle a few yards away, she left him with a saucy smile and one thought: "I love a challenge, Jackson, but don't draw this out any longer than you have to. You snooze, you lose."

Angelica sat at her desk, wondering how much longer it was going to take to wear Jackson down.

She'd talked a good game with him, full of sass and sensual bravado, but she wasn't sure her self-esteem could take much more of his polite indifference. She'd flirted full force with the man for a full year—progressively taking her strategy up a notch with each encounter. The way she saw it, in a couple of weeks, she'd have to strip out of her panties and toss them in his face for him to get a friggin' clue. What was the problem? She'd done her homework. She knew he was straight and he wasn't involved with anyone at the moment. Was it simply a case of no chemistry on his end? Was Angelica not pretty enough, intriguing enough or hot enough? Just once, she hoped that Jackson would look at her with the same fascination he'd shown that crazy chick who had stormed the newsroom the day before and dumped pasta all over his desk. Angelica fumed, then tried appeasing herself with the thought that she'd finally finagled a way to spend some time with him outside the newsroom. She supposed joining him and Abigail for dinner was progress. Abigail was nice enough and a romantic at heart. Maybe Angelica could even convince Abigail to make herself scarce before their evening was over.

Angelica jumped when Vince Lomax appeared out of nowhere, snatching her from her reverie.

"You really oughta give it up," he said as a rakish smile spread across his bronze face. His straight black hair was slicked back in a ponytail, a fashion statement which was more about the Native American half of his heritage and less about aping cheesy Steven

Segal. Razor stubble shadowed his strong, angular jaw. The fluorescent lighting reflected off the small silver hoop piercing his left earlobe.

"Give up what?" Angelica asked, not bothering to hide her rancor.

"It's getting kind of pathetic, you know." Vince was one of the *Tribune*'s top photographers, the workplace lothario and now the unrelenting pain in Angelica's ass. He'd been traveling through Europe on sabbatical for a year, but since he'd returned a month ago he'd made a sport of pestering Angelica.

Angelica signed on her computer and busied herself tapping the keyboard. "I have no idea what you're talking about."

Vince leaned against the left wall of her cubicle and fiddled with the camera dangling from the nylon loop around his neck. "I think you do, but if I must spell it out for you, it's the way you keep throwing yourself at Jackson." He tsk-tsked her. "Everybody but you seems to know it's a lost cause. You're not our boy's type."

Angelica stopped typing and turned her chair to face him. "And how do you know Jackson's type?" she said tartly, crossing her arms across her breasts. "Have you tried finagling a date with him yourself and he turned you down?"

"You're funny," Vince said with a deep, gravelly laugh, a laugh so condescending she wanted to sink her acrylic nails in his carotid artery. "Now you know our Vince ain't hardly swinging that way. Jackson's all buttoned-down and conservative. Don't get me wrong, I think he's a cool brotha and we've thrown down a few brewskies together after hours. But he's not audacious enough…" Vince leisurely scanned the length of Angelica's legs, "to know how to appreciate a woman like you, Angie."

Angelica was surprised and displeased by her reaction to the look Vince had given her. Her skin actually goose bumped in pleasure until she reminded herself that he was the newsroom player. A real cad. A sleazy, no-good-hit-it-and-quit-it ho-hopper to be exact. *Tribune* gossip had it that he'd not only bedded every unattached young woman in the newsroom, but he'd worked his way through the circulation and advertising departments, too. He'd even gotten busy with a few married ones. And hadn't Angelica even heard he kept souvenirs—kinky videos and photos of these sexual encounters? "I don't allow anyone to call me Angie—not even my parents. It's An-ge-li-ca," she snapped.

"So, I hear you're a real sucker for…seafood." Only Vince could make seafood sound like something whispered on one of those 900 talk-dirty-to-me phone lines.

"And your point is…?"

"I hear you've been trying to convince a certain someone to take you to Cesaro's. I've been curious about the place myself. Maybe we could go together."

Angelica replied with laughter. "You must be kidding. Like a date?"

"Yes, as in two people—you and me—getting dressed up and driving in an automobile to an establishment where we'll converse while we get sustenance." He mimicked shoveling food inside his mouth, as if he were explaining an earthling ritual to a Martian.

"That's the most ridiculous thing I've ever heard."

"Why?" Vince asked, hardly rankled by her rude reaction. "I just know…" he blatantly ogled her boobs, "we'd be real good together."

Angelica craned her neck to peek around Vince. Jackson rose from his chair and shrugged into his sport jacket before heading toward the exit.

Vince followed her gaze, then shook his head. "Angie baby, you're wasting your time mooning over that one."

"And so are you," she told him. "And it's An-ge-li-ca."

"Why do you have to play me like this?" He winced and brought his hands to his heart in mock agony.

"Because I refuse to be another notch on your Nikon. You might as well get lost, Lomax."

Vince dropped his pained act and gave her a knowing, lopsided grin. "Hmmp, hmmp, hmmp. So you gonna make this brotha work for it, huh? I can dig it. You know what they say about anything worth having. If you need me, I'll be in the studio darkroom. If you get lonely, you can join me." He backed away with a wink and lewd grin. "And remember that dark-room has a lock."

Angelica shuddered.

Damn Vince. If he hadn't lingered around her desk aggravating and distracting her, she could've caught up with Jackson and found out where he was headed, maybe even convinced him to join her for a quick bite in the *Tribune*'s cafeteria.

Angelica knew she had gone beyond pushy with Jackson. The subtle, demure approach she'd initially attempted had been a total bust. She had been danger-ously close to veering over into the dreaded "one of the guys" category with him. Jackson had even started slapping her on the back and telling her how "hot" he thought celebrities like Halle Berry and Janet Jackson were. Angelica shuddered at the thought. She wanted him to feel comfortable enough to share things with her. But she wanted to be his friend and lover. To that end, she'd sexed up her look and ratcheted up her flir-tation several notches. It really wasn't her usual style, but more of a desperate role-playing maneuver to pique his interest. It hadn't had the desired effect—yet—but it assured he would not forget she was a woman. Being the aggressor had been hell on her self-image, but anything worth having was worth putting in an extra effort for. Jackson was more than worthy. He represented everything she wanted in a man. Not only was he smart, handsome, classy, and sexy as hell, but he was a genuinely nice guy. And these days, the nice part topped her manhunt list. She'd had her share of insensitive bad boys. It was high time she flipped the script.

Angelica had seen Jackson in action numerous times with bereaved people who'd come to the newsroom to deliver photos for their loved ones' obituaries. Some would drift near his cubicle because it was near the obit clerk's desk. Some had been so distraught they'd purge to anyone within earshot. Though it wasn't part of Jackson's job, he would often console them just by expressing interest in the person who'd passed away.

Angelica finished her hosiery piece, then gave it a thorough inspection before punching the computer key that would send it to the copydesk. She checked the clock. Eleven-fifteen a.m. It was still early. Jackson was sure to return before the workday ended. She hoped to get another chance to see him before the sun went down.

CHAPTER 4

After lunch, Jackson spent the rest of the afternoon scouting a couple of eateries on the west end that he'd considered adding to his review list. Just before seven he arrived at the Silver Spoon. The place was busier than the previous night, but it wasn't a full house by a long shot. A muscular guy of medium height wearing small wire-rimmed glasses glared at Jackson from the host station near the front entrance.

Daphne spotted Jackson immediately and greeted him with a warm smile. "Never mind him." She tipped her head toward the bespectacled guy. "That's just Troy. Savannah's expecting you." She slipped into the back to fetch her boss.

Savannah appeared wearing a soft peach sleeveless dress that flattered her flawless cinnamon skin. "Hello, Jackson. Join me in my office."

Jackson followed as Savannah led the way and he couldn't help admiring the trim waist which underscored the voluptuousness of her womanly curves. "So how was business today?"

"Better, but still nothing to brag about," Savannah replied as they both stepped inside her smallish office. She took the seat behind her desk, then encouraged Jackson to take the chair positioned across from it. She reached inside a drawer and removed a legal pad, then grabbed a pen and obviously poised herself to take copious notes. "Okay, shoot. Spill all the secrets and suggestions you believe will make the Silver Spoon a smashing success." Her manner was all business.

"Well, actually, I was kinda hoping we could chat first. You know, get to know one another."

"Chat?" Savannah asked, as if the idea had never occurred to her. "Oh, yeah, right." She bobbed her head.

"Tell me about your background." Jackson cleared his throat. "Your background in the restaurant business, I mean, how and why you got started and tell me about any training and experience you've had."

Savannah placed her pen on her desk and relaxed against her chair. What she revealed during that next half hour confirmed Jackson's hunch. She'd been a business administration major in college, but her restaurant experience had been limited to the stints she'd worked at various eating establishments. She'd been everything from a cashier to a hostess, but had never held a management position. She'd mistakenly believed her enthusiasm for the food service business would push her through all the rough patches she might encounter as a restaurateur. The restaurant business was damn hard and competitive. It required more than unyielding passion. Even seasoned owners couldn't always guarantee that their newest ventures would make it past that critical first year or two.

Savannah had done a decent job so far with her paperwork, given her lack of experience. She'd maintained accurate records, including extremely detailed weekly cost and profit spreadsheets. The location she'd selected was top rate and the restaurant space itself was spacious and attractive. She'd recently revamped her initial marketing approach. The revision was sound. Jackson listened intently before he ventured to offer advice on paring down her too-long and too-elaborate menu and increasing the efficiency of her service staff.

A little less than three hours later, Daphne knocked, then poked her head inside the office to remind Savannah that closing time had drawn near.

Jackson used the break to stand and stretch. "Near closing? Where did the time go?"

Savannah glanced at the pages of notes she'd taken. "I have to admit you've given me a lot to think about, Jackson. These are some fantastic ideas. I'm not sure where to begin."

"Just realize that the type of success you're going for won't happen overnight. It's going to take more methodical planning, adjustments and time."

Jackson reached for the sport jacket he'd removed and hung on the back of his chair.

"You're leaving? Can I interest you in some dessert and coffee on the house?" Savannah asked. Then quickly she added, "The desserts aren't made here. So you're safe."

"I know they're delicious. If you'll recall, in the review I wrote that the cheesecake and apple pie were worth a try."

"It slipped my mind, since your praise was so spare," Savannah retaliated dryly.

"So what's the story on your desserts?"

"A nice old retired lady named Eloise Johnson whips up all of our sweets."

"Well, good for Eloise. Does she have any other specialties outside of dessert? You might want to pick her brain on a few other dishes."

Savannah slapped her hand to her forehead as if she'd experienced an epiphany. "Hey, you might be onto something there. I can't believe I never thought of asking Eloise about anything else— besides desserts—though she did bring me chicken soup when I was ill. Very delicious, homemade chicken soup, I might add. She's a dear friend, but I hadn't really thought about using her as a menu consultant."

"If she can whip up entrees as delicious as her cheesecake and apple pie, Savannah, you just might have stumbled upon the secret weapon that will make the Silver Spoon a serious contender. You said she was retired. Think she'd be open to sharing some of her recipes or maybe training your cooks?"

"It can't hurt to ask now, can it?" Savannah replied. "So, can I interest you in a slice of Eloise's dessert of the day? Something she calls cherry torte." Her features softened with a wistful expression. "It's simply divine. It has plump sweet cherries, whipped cream and a melt-in-your-mouth sugar and walnut crumb crust."

"You've convinced me," Jackson replied as he trailed Savannah out of the office. He took a seat at one of the tables at the front of the empty dining room.

The Silver Spoon staff prepared to depart. Savannah called out to the waitress named Daphne, "Before you leave, could you be a dear and get us a couple of orders of that cherry torte and two cups of coffee. You know how I take mine."

"Black, please," Jackson told the waitress.

"Sure thing." Daphne turned to Savannah. "Oh, I almost forgot. Troy said he had to step out for a bit to take care of something. But he promised to return in time to go over the day's receipts with you. He said not to even think about stepping foot out of this restaurant without him." Daphne slipped back inside the kitchen.

"This Troy seems very protective of you," Jackson noted tightly.

"He's no more protective of me than I am of him."

"Oh." Jackson pursed his lips as jealousy pricked him.

"We're very close, ya know." Savannah leaned forward as if she were studying his reaction.

"Is that right?" he replied with a frosty edge.

"Yes, he's my right hand, my confidante, my manager…"

Disenchanted that Savannah was obviously spoken for, Jackson shifted uneasily in his seat and checked his watch. Maybe he'd skip the coffee and dessert after all.

"And my brother," she revealed with what looked like a *gotcha!* smile.

Relieved, Jackson's appetite returned when Daphne reappeared with a tray containing two cups of coffee, generous servings of the torte and silverware.

"Anything else before I head out?" Daphne asked.

Savannah reached for a fork. "No, thanks, Daphne. Just leave the tray on the next table. I'll take care of it."

"See ya tomorrow, Savannah, and nice seeing you again, Jackson," Daphne said just before gathering her belongings for her departure.

Jackson sampled a bite of his dessert. "This is delicious. Even better than that cheesecake I had. And it was pretty darn hard to beat that cheesecake."

"Told ya." Savannah was already on her second mouthful.

When the door closed behind Daphne, the restaurant was suddenly pin-drop quiet save for the clinking of their forks against china plates.

Eating that slice of torte simply called attention to lips that looked way too soft and cushy to resist, Jackson thought. The neckline of Savannah's linen dress scooped just enough to hint at soft, brown mounds rising from it. Jackson wished he could wedge his tongue where the small clover-shaped pendant dangled from a gold chain. It nestled between the slopes of her cleavage.

The fact that they were obviously alone emboldened Jackson. What was to stop him from making a move? From leaning closer and venturing to taste the cherry torte on her lips? He considered going for it until his better judgment reined him in. A premature move such as that could ruin everything before it even started. *Pace yourself, man.* He was here to help Savannah, not hit on her.

At least, not yet.

The flicker of interest he thought he'd detected in her eyes didn't guarantee that she was available. Though some women weren't free to order, they still liked to scan the menu.

And Jackson wasn't completely sure he was ready to follow through on any moves toward physical intimacy, anyway. The dream last night had given him hope, but it had been months since he'd been with a woman. Maybe that's why he felt a heightened sensitivity when he was near Savannah.

Everything about her registered with startling acuity. From the ethereal glow of her cinnamon-colored skin to her uniquely glorious fragrance. He was sure it hadn't come from some perfume bottle. It was just the essence of Savannah. He couldn't seem to tear his gaze from her mouth.

"So, do you have other siblings? Or is it just you and Troy?" Jackson tried to make conversation to control his lustful thoughts.

"Just the two of us."

"A significant other?" he ventured boldly.

"Nope, not anymore. Free and single and ready to mingle." Savannah chuckled, then added, "What about you? You have any brothers and sisters?"

"Yeah, got a brother. A twin actually, named Julian."

"Really? When I was younger I always thought it would be so cool to have a twin."

"I know what you're thinking. Someone to swap places with to fool teachers and friends, right? Well, we weren't that kind of twins."

"Not identical?" she asked before breaking off another piece of torte with her fork.

"No, fraternal. We resemble, but not so much that we could fool anybody with decent eyesight who has seen us standing side by side." Jackson added with a laugh, "For one thing, I've got about two extra inches on him, which galls him to no end. And I do my part to rub it in by calling him Shorty every now and then." Jackson sipped his coffee.

"Shorty? You're about what? Six-three? Six-four?"

"Six-three."

Savannah swallowed the torte in her mouth, then added, "So Julian is six-one. That's only short by NBA standards."

"Julian and I are very close, but we do enjoy giving each other a hard time every now and then. When we were teens he could dance up a storm and he always teased me about having no rhythm on the dance floor. Then I'd tell him the running man and the humpty dance was for wusses."

When Savannah laughed again, he realized how addicted he'd become to that sound.

She finished her last bite of torte, then reached for a napkin in the holder to dab against her lips. She gave him a soft look. "I can't believe what a difference twenty-four hours can make. Just yesterday I was thinking of a thousand and one different ways for you to die a slow, agonizing death. Now here we are laughing over coffee and cherry torte."

"So, is that your roundabout way of admitting you're sorta-kinda glad I called and that you sorta-kinda enjoy my company?" Jackson felt a grin tugging at his lips. He leaned closer to Savannah, captivated by her silky-lashed, brown eyes.

"Is this your way of letting me know that you're sorta-kinda thinking of kissing me, Mr. DeWitt?"

"If I were, would you do more than sorta-kinda kiss me back?"

"Only if you're more than sorta-kinda available."

"Oh, I'm very available for you, Savannah. So how about it?"

When she moistened her lips, Jackson had his answer. He'd leaned in closer still, tilting her chin up, when Troy swooshed from the back through the swinging doors.

Savannah jerked away from Jackson, pushed to her feet and gathered their empty dessert dishes and silverware.

"Hey, sis, sorry I'm late," Troy said. "Sharon had a little problem with a flat tire and it was taking AAA forever to show up."

"Sharon?" Savannah placed their dishes on the tray she'd lifted from another table.

"You know, the aerobics instructor I met at the gym. We've been dating for two weeks now. I told you about her."

"Don't fault me for not remembering her. It's hard to keep up with all of your women." Suddenly fidgety, Savannah lost her grip and the tray in her hands wobbled a bit. Jackson deftly caught it by the edge and steadied it for her. "I don't believe you two have been officially introduced. Troy, this is Jackson, Jackson Dewitt, from the *Cincinnati Tribune*. Jackson, this is my brother Troy."

Jackson extended his hand for a shake. "Nice to meet you, Troy."

"Jackson." Troy offered a curt nod, but pointedly ignored Jackson's hand.

Jackson chose not to take offense, presuming the chilly response had more to the do with the scathing review he'd written on the Silver Spoon than anything else. If Savannah could warm up and give him a second chance, he figured Troy would, too, eventually, given enough time.

Jackson checked his watch again, then buried his hands inside his pant pockets. "It is getting late."

"Don't rush off on my account." Troy couldn't sound more insincere.

"I'd better get going and let you two go over those receipts Daphne mentioned earlier," Jackson said. "Thanks for the coffee and dessert, Savannah. Both were delicious."

Troy snorted with obvious disbelief.

"Yes, delicious," Jackson repeated, trying not to let Troy get to him.

"And thank you for all the information and ideas for this place. I'm going to get started on some of those things we discussed first thing tomorrow, starting with having a chat with Eloise."

"What about Eloise?" Troy piped up.

"I'll fill you in later," Savannah replied as she escorted Jackson to the front door, where they stood awkwardly eyeing each other.

How Jackson wanted to pick up where he and Savannah had left off before her brother returned. But a first kiss was too special to turn into a spectator sport. Troy stared at them while they exchanged their goodbyes.

"Thanks again for giving this arrangement a shot," Jackson said.

"And thank you for offering. I still can't believe you actually came back here."

Jackson opened the door and stepped outside. He caught Savannah by the wrist and tugged her with him, then closed the door. Privacy at last!

Savannah smiled up at him, pressing her back against the glass front of the Silver Spoon. Jackson braced both arms against the exterior of the building, caging her in.

"So, are we putting that review behind us and starting with a clean slate—once and for all?" He bent to brush the tip of his nose against hers.

"I suppose."

He dropped one hand from the glass and traced the soft skin on her cheek. "I can't retract that review. But if there's anything else I can do to help get this place on track, just ask. I want you to be successful."

"And why is that so important to you?" Savannah gazed up at him intently. "You hardly know me."

"But I know more today than I did yesterday and I'd love to learn still more. I think you're fascinating, Savannah, and despite what I wrote in that review, after hearing your story, I'm very impressed with what you've managed to accomplish here so far. I mean, you have your very own restaurant. Not many people get that far. You didn't just dream it, you made it happen."

"There's no limit to what one can do with a lot of chutzpah and a healthy divorce settlement," Savannah said with a self-deprecating chuckle. Then her hands came to rest against his chest. The heat of her touch seared through his cotton shirt.

She'd provided him with the perfect segue to reveal what he'd heard about her ex-husband's machinations, but the timing couldn't have been worse. Not when her palms were molded against his pecs and her plump sexy lips beckoned, sending ripples of desire through him. An erection pressed against the zipper of his pants. That had happened more in the past two days since he'd met Savannah than it had in the past seven months. They'd closed the scant inches between them and Jackson was a second from claiming her lips when Troy jerked the front door open.

"Savannah, time to get to those receipts. I told Sharon I'd swing by again before she turned in for the night," Troy said.

Savannah pushed away from the restaurant's glass front and sighed with impatience. "Troy!"

"What? I promised her I'd come right back," Troy explained. "And it's not what you're thinking, either. It's not a booty call. I had to leave after fixing her flat tire to get back to the restaurant to close with you. But another tire has a slow leak."

"And you're going to fix this slow leak, as you call it, tonight?" Savannah asked as if she wasn't convinced.

"She has an attached, lighted garage—not a problem," Troy insisted.

Savannah turned to Jackson. "I guess this is goodnight."

"Goodnight, Savannah." Reluctantly Jackson turned to head for his black Acura in the Silver Spoon's lighted parking lot. Midway, he paused and tossed over his shoulder, "Oh, can I call you tomorrow?"

Savannah smiled and replied with the moxie he found irresistible, "You'd better."

Savannah watched Jackson navigate his car out of the parking lot and down the narrow street until the night swallowed the taillights.

When she stepped back inside the Silver Spoon, Troy pinned her with a hard look. "So what's this about Eloise?"

"Jackson and I were talking about our dessert menu and he had this great idea," Savannah explained as she moved toward her office. "While we're looking for a head chef, why not bring Eloise in as a cooking consultant? You know her desserts are to die for, right? I'd never considered asking Eloise what else she might be good at. If her other dishes are as mouth-watering as her desserts and soup, then we might have stumbled upon someone who can make the Silver Spoon a standout restaurant. She could be our secret weapon."

"So you're making significant decisions about the place without my input?" Troy sniffed as he fell in step with her.

Savannah heard the indignation in his voice. She stopped, reached for his hands and turned to face him. "Troy, it's not like that. I'm running it by you now. I do want to know what you think of this idea."

"But it sounds as if you've already made up your mind to talk to Eloise about this. So you don't really want my opinion. You're just informing me of what you've already decided to do."

"Yes, I got overly excited about the prospect of talking to Eloise. And that's the only decision I've made so far. I can't believe I never thought of consulting with her before."

"So hanging out with Jackson obviously has your creative entrepreneurial juices flowing." Sarcasm threaded Troy's words, but Savannah refused to take offense and pull rank. After all, the Silver Spoon was her baby. She didn't need Troy's approval for anything, but she knew his reaction stemmed from an overprotective instinct that they both shared. He would need time to adjust to the idea of Savannah working with Jackson.

She wasn't even sure how to label what was developing between her and her new associate. For

lack of a better word, she'd go with "arrangement."
Her brother was going to need time to adjust to her
"arrangement" with Jackson, a man whose motives
he still didn't trust. Beyond the fact that she was
wildly attracted to the man, Savannah wasn't so sure
about him either. Were there unspoken ulterior
motives for helping her out?

CHAPTER 5

Jackson phoned Savannah the first thing the next morning. As soon as he wrapped up his duties at one of the review restaurants of the week, he made his way to the Silver Spoon, where he and Savannah tossed around more ideas on how to improve her restaurant.

The pair saw each other every night for the next three weeks, but having Troy hovering made attempting anything beyond business difficult. Jackson's frequent visits to the restaurant did little to ease Troy's obvious suspicions.

The weekend of his niece's Sunbeam Girl troop meeting couldn't arrive fast enough. The bargain they'd struck for Savannah to speak to the little girls became Jackson's first opportunity to get her away from the Silver Spoon and that overprotective brother of hers.

After a delightful thirty-minute talk about the Silver Spoon and why it had been her life-long dream, Savannah left the rest of her presentation open to take questions from the group of pre-teen girls, who'd huddled around her at the community center. The girls, including his niece Sasha, appeared genuinely charmed by Savannah. That hadn't come as a surprise to Jackson. He'd had a feeling they'd enjoy her as much as he had the past three weeks.

There was an innate warmth and effervescence about Savannah that drew people near. Jackson had noted the exchange between Savannah and that elderly gentleman in her restaurant that night Jackson had shown up under the guise of returning her serving dish. The man had sat alone perched over a bowl of soup. At one point he'd been so still Jackson had wondered if he'd dozed off sitting upright. But the old man's posture had snapped erect and his face lit up when he caught sight of Savannah. Jackson wondered if he was sporting the same telltale sign of one who'd been thoroughly captivated by the woman.

Doris Fondren, the Sunbeam troop's adult adviser, moved to the front of the room to inform the girls that there was time for two more questions before they'd have to proceed with their official troop meeting. The group groaned their disapproval.

"But we've hardly had a chance to ask Ms. Savannah all our questions," a little girl sporting a mop of skinny microbraids whined. The rest of the group chimed in its agreement.

"An hour of questions is plenty of time," Ms. Fondren said. "Besides, I'm sure Ms. Savannah has other things to do today. Remember she has a restaurant to run, little ladies. Maybe Ms. Savannah can come back to see us sometime if her schedule permits."

Ms. Fondren looked to Savannah, who was obviously pleasantly overwhelmed by the chorus of "would-you-could-you?" and "pretty please!"

The smile that Savannah had worn the past hour and a half grew more vibrant. "You girls sure it's me you want to see again? Or it is the fresh-baked chocolate chip and peanut butter cookies Ms. Eloise sent?" she teased.

"It's you, Ms. Savannah!" a little freckled redheaded girl piped up. "We'd like to hear that story again about how those mean ol' boys wouldn't let you join their tree house club and how you got them to change their minds when you set up a neighborhood lemonade stand and forced them to pay twice the price of your other customers. That was smart! You taught them what true girl power is!"

"All right! You've convinced me. I'll check with Ms. Fondren to find out when I can come to visit your troop again. How's that?" Savannah said her goodbyes, then joined Jackson, who stood admiring her from the back of the room.

"That went well," Jackson said. "I had a hunch you'd be a huge hit."

"They're such sweet little girls and so smart! Did you hear some of those questions? I'd better watch my back. Before I know it some of them will be grown, running their own restaurants and giving Ms. Savannah a run for her money," she said, still hopped up on the good vibes that had flowed from her captive young audience. "That little Sasha is something else."

"Like father, like daughter," Jackson replied as they walked toward the exit. "She's definitely a daddy's girl. All about the benjamins, baby." He chuckled. "Sorry, I didn't know she would get so persistent with her questions about your finances."

"I think all she really wanted to know is if I made more money than Britney Spears. And we both know the answer to that," Savannah replied with a chuckle as they crossed the parking lot to Jackson's car.

"I liked the all-dessert-all-the-time suggestion from the little girl with the bifocals." Jackson opened the passenger side door for Savannah. As she climbed in he admired her shapely legs.

Once settled into the driver's seat, Jackson fitted his key in the ignition, though he was in no hurry to take her back to the Silver Spoon. "You say Troy is keeping an eye on things for you the rest of the day and evening?"

Savannah hesitated, then slanted him a look. A shadow of a grin played on her lips. "That depends. What did you have in mind?"

"Is that a yes?" Jackson smiled back as he cranked the engine.

"It's a maybe."

"So you're going to make me take charge of the situation?" Jackson reached across her lap to open his glove compartment. "The cell is inside. Phone your brother and tell him you're going to be late, very late."

🐦

"Thanks for being so understanding about taking this detour," Jackson said to Savannah as their elevator ascended to the twentieth floor of the *Tribune* building.

"No complaints since I had no idea where you were taking me in the first place." Savannah watched the light above the door illuminate numbers with each passing floor.

Jackson patted the front pocket of his sport jacket. "I can't believe how absentminded I've been lately."

"So are you going give me a hint or what?" Savannah smiled.

"You'll see soon enough." When the elevator stopped at the twentieth floor Jackson lifted a hand to cup her elbow. He guided her off into the entryway leading to the newsroom. "This way."

The most innocent touches seemed to set off sparks along the surface of Savannah's skin. As she followed him to his desk, she couldn't help remembering the last time she'd crashed the *Tribune*, hopped on anger. That day the newsroom had been packed with people who'd witnessed her little retaliation.

This Saturday afternoon, fewer people milled about the newsroom, but her cheeks flushed when she recalled how irrationally she'd behaved during her previous visit. Maybe no one would recognize her as the pasta-wielding psycho.

At his desk Jackson unlocked the middle drawer, removed an envelope and presented it to her. "Here they are."

"What?" Savannah asked.

"Open the envelope and find out." Jackson's lips stretched into a warm smile.

"Tickets?" Savannah said, parting the folds of the envelope.

"Yes, for *Aida*."

"Both tickets are for me?" Savannah's eyes went wide. "How did you know?"

"During one of our conversations about the Out & About section you mentioned how much you enjoyed the feature our arts reporter did on the show. And how intrigued you were about it."

Savannah searched her memory. "Maybe, but we discussed a lot of stories in that section besides your restaurant reviews."

"One thing you'll come to learn about me, Savannah, is I'm not one of those men who zones out when a women speaks. I listen, I mean, really listen to everything. Dreams, hopes, desires and wishes are my specialty." Jackson reached for her hand and lifted it. His lips grazed her knuckles. Delightful tingles originating at her fingers scattered

over her body. "I want to know everything about
you."

"As in dogs versus cats, boxers versus briefs, Pepsi
vs. Coke—"

"Fast versus slow. Top versus bottom," he replied,
taking his voice down a notch in a way that made
her giddy with yearning.

When Savannah gazed up into Jackson's hooded
eyes, she could almost forget they weren't alone.
Almost, until the sound of someone noisily clearing
a throat broke the beguiling force simmering
between them.

A tall, beautiful woman with hair so black and
shiny it looked like spun onyx approached them. She
wore a black low-cut tank top tucked neatly into a
too-short denim shirt. A pair of funky platforms
adorned her feet. She looked vaguely familiar to
Savannah.

"Angelica," Jackson said with a note of surprise.
"What are you doing here on a Saturday? Isn't this
your off day?"

Savannah found herself scrutinizing how Jackson
and this glamazon interacted. Women like this
Angelica, who obviously used their sexual assets as a
weapon, tended to make Savannah feel dumpier and
frumpier than usual, but she refused to let insecurity
get the best of her. However, Savannah couldn't help
wishing she'd slipped on her pair of pumps with a
vixen heel instead of the modest mules she was

wearing that did absolutely nothing to enhance her stubby legs.

"Hello, Jackson!" Angelica threw Savannah a quick chilly look before shifting her attention back to Jackson again. "I had a shoot today. We're still photographing the latest pool and beachwear accessories in the studio to go along with that swimsuit layout we shot poolside at the Martin mansion a few weeks ago."

"Why didn't you just shoot all of it at the mansion at same time?" Jackson asked.

"Some of the swimsuits and hats we wanted to feature hadn't arrived yet and the mansion's owner, Bryce Martin, has been out of town for the past three weeks. We weren't sure when he'd return and that deadline is still looming."

"I know that this big summer fashion tabloid is usually the splashiest of the year," Jackson said. "Sounds like you pulled out all the stops this year to get the Martin mansion."

"It wasn't so hard," Angelica added. "Prescott had the hookup."

"Prescott is our publisher," Jackson told Savannah, who didn't bother to reveal that the Martin mansion used to be her home.

When had Bryce started opening the place for photo shoots? Then she recalled that the *Tribune* often featured the swankiest residences, halls and hotels in those shoots. Bryce probably felt as if he'd arrived and garnered some sort of tacit high-society seal of approval when he'd been asked if his estate was available. Her thoughts then moved to something else that had puzzled her for the past three weeks. Bryce hadn't merely given up harassing her, as she'd hoped. He hadn't called to mock her about that review because he'd been out of town all this time on business. It was possible he hadn't seen it and maybe he never would, she thought with satisfaction.

"Excuse my manners," Jackson said. "You two have seen each other, but you haven't been officially introduced."

"The noodle woman, right?" Angelica asked, her condescending tone ringing clear.

"Her name is Savannah Jacobs," Jackson revealed with a light chuckle. "Savannah, this is Angelica Alexander, the *Tribune*'s very talented fashion editor."

Savannah extended her hand despite the unfriendly look Angelica was giving her. It was quite obvious Jackson's coworker was pissed. While Jackson didn't appear unnerved by Angelica's presence, Savannah wondered what the story was between these two.

"Savannah, I don't know if you noticed, but that show is for today," Jackson said.

"Today?" Savannah searched the tickets for the show time. "Hey, why didn't you tell me it was a matinee? That doesn't give me much time to draft someone to join me," she teased, knowing full well that had been Jackson's plan all along. "These are my tickets, right? To do with as I please?" She blocked out the evil looks Angelica was giving her.

"True, you can invite anyone you want," Jackson played along.

"Hmmm, let me think." Savannah performed her little act to the hilt. "Troy's holding down the fort at the Silver Spoon…Daphne's working this shift… Let's see, who else? Who else? Eloise is taking care of her great-grandson today….Who else? Who else?" Savannah pursed her lips for a long pensive minute. "And my friend Wanda is out of town on a business trip…"

"Did you see the clock? You'll get to the Aronoff Center in the nick of time only if you leave now," he prodded.

"All right, I guess I'm stuck with you, Jackson," Savannah replied with a phony reluctant sigh. "It's a shame to let a perfectly good ticket to *Aida* go to waste."

"You two have tickets to *Aida*?" Angelica asked.

"Yes, Jackson here bought them for me. Wasn't that sweet of him?" Savannah really wasn't trying to rub it in, but she could tell from Angelica's pinched expression that the leggy fashion editor had taken it that way.

"I didn't know you were a musical theatre fan, Jackson," Angelica bit out. "Seems I recall trying to coax you with two tickets to *South Pacific* and you turned me down flat."

"I couldn't leave work that night because I had deadlines out the wah-zoo that day," Jackson explained. "We'd better get going. We don't want to be late." Jackson caught Savannah by the waist. "Enjoy the rest of your weekend, Angelica. Don't work too hard. And I'll get with you and Abigail about Cesaro's…um…maybe some time next week."

"Nice meeting you, Angelica," Savannah called over her shoulder, as Jackson steered her toward the exit.

❦

Angelica cringed and watched the happy couple board the elevator. She clenched her hands into tight fists. Her acrylic nails jabbed the tender flesh of her palms. If she gnashed her teeth any harder her molars would crumble.

She heard Vince behind her. "Told ya. What more do you need to see to get a clue, Angie?"

"Why aren't you in the studio finishing those shots?" Angelica snapped.

"Because I've shot everything you brought back to the studio for me. I came out here to find out what was taking you so long to return with those straw hats you left to fetch, remember? And what do I find? You standing out here with steam practically shooting out of your ears 'cause Jackson has obviously met someone who captured his buttoned-down fancy."

Angelica's eyeballs stung and she knew tears threatened to fall. But she'd never cried over any man and she didn't plan to start now—even for a great catch like Jackson DeWitt. For once she was too emotionally exhausted to fight with Vince. She dropped into the closest chair, the one at Jackson's desk, to get her bearings. The faint scent of Jackson's cologne lingered. She looked up at the scruffy photographer, who sported blue jeans that had faded to white in the most interesting locations. It wasn't the first time Angelica had noticed he had a great body—lean and rippled, but strong. Then there was that feral quality about him that she supposed could be sexy to some women who loved the challenge of bad boys. She wasn't one of them, she had to remind herself when Vince placed a hand on her shoulder in a consoling gesture. But despite her better judgment, she leaned into the comfort he'd offered.

"You can do so much better with a man who really wants to be with you, Angie," Vince said, squeezing her shoulder.

"And you think that man is you?" Angelica asked with a mirthless chuckle.

"Why do you think I keep sniffing around? Why do you think I volunteered to do studio shoots of fashion accessories, of all things. You know I don't usually do froufrou photography and on my day off, no less. That should be a clue-and-a-half for you."

"You volunteered to shoot pool-side accessories to spend time with me?" Angelica lifted a skeptical brow.

"Yes. You're one sexy lady," Vince said. "A guy would have to have some serious screws loose not to want to explore the possibilities."

"And you're ready to explore?"

"Call me Christopher Columbus, babe," Vince said with a wink. "C'mon, after we finish up here, let me take you to dinner, Angie. I'll spring for Cesaro's. You could use some cheering up. You go home and put on one of your hottest dresses. I guarantee to make it a night you won't forget."

Angelica's ego had taken a beating after watching Jackson fawn all over that crazy pasta-packing chick. And to think, Angelica had spent a whole year chasing him only to get rebuffed every time. To add insult to injury, she'd had to stand there and watch him practically beg that woman to let him accompany her to that show. If that wasn't enough to knock some sense into Angelica, there was no hope for her at all. From that day forward, she swore on her most expensive pair of Manolo Blahniks that she was done jocking Jackson DeWitt for good. He'd had his chance with her and he'd blown it. Next!

"What do you say, Angie?" Vince prompted, charming her with a big gleaming smile.

"It's An-ge-li-ca," she said.

"Angelica. Happy? Now will you please have dinner with me?"

Before Jackson departed he mentioned getting back to Angelica and Abigail next week about their dinner at Cesaro's. Announcing that she'd already been to the restaurant and had a fantastic time with Vince would be a grand way to show Jackson she wasn't sitting around waiting on him to wake up and smell the iced mocha latte anymore. She'd moved on!

"I hear Cesaro's has the freshest seafood in town. I promise you all the lobster you can eat," Vince said. "So what do you say?"

"I say… you can pick me up at seven," Angelica replied, treating Vince to his first genuine smile from her.

CHAPTER 6

Daylight had dissolved into dusk when the curtain closed on *Aida*.

"The show was wonderful," Savannah said as she and Jackson strolled to his car parked in the lot adjacent to the Aronoff Center. "I've been wanting to see this one ever since I heard Elton John and Tim Rice penned the score and the lyrics."

"So you weren't turned off by the fact that it was a Disney production?" Jackson led the way to the passenger side so he could open the door and assist Savannah.

"No, not at all. With the success of *The Lion King* I think Disney has more than proven it can produce a decent Broadway musical." Savannah made herself comfortable on the front seat.

"From what I heard initial attempts to bring the show to the stage were plagued with problems—collapsing sets, injured cast members, mixed early reviews." Jackson slipped in and started the engine.

"I don't care about that. They've obviously worked out the kinks and all I took in were the eye-popping sets, grand costumes, great music and very romantic epic storytelling." Savannah's voice floated on a wistful note. "That was so thoughtful of you to get the tickets. Thank you."

"You've thanked me plenty already, but I'm not done with you yet," Jackson said, throwing her a knee-weakening grin.

"You mean there's more?"

"Yes, indeed."

"Where are we headed? Am I dressed all right?"

Jackson took his eyes off the road and skimmed the simple white dress that accentuated her curves. "You look beautiful, if I haven't told you already. But there's no dress code where we're going."

Savannah felt her face heating beneath his dreamy gaze. "Eyes front and center, dude." A light chuckle escaped. "We don't want you crashing into that Toyota half a car length ahead."

Jackson complied. The man definitely had a way of making her feel like the most exquisite creature he'd ever encountered.

And that was just as much of a turn-on as his masculine good looks.

"Jackson," Savannah ventured slowly. "I've been meaning to ask…about Angelica…I don't mean to pry—"

"Yes, you do, but go ahead, fire away," he said with a teasing grin.

"For a minute, it felt a little awkward, the way she was looking at you and me. What's the story there?"

"There's no story. Angelica is a colleague. She has a bit of a crush."

"A bit of a crush?" Savannah slanted a skeptical look at him.

"Okay, so she flirts, but it's all in fun."

"And do you flirt back?"

"I like Angelica a lot, but I'm not interested in her that way."

"And why not? She's a beautiful woman."

"True, but it takes more than looks to catch my eye and besides, I don't think it's a smart idea to date a co-worker. And what about you? You mentioned that a divorce settlement helped you secure the Silver Spoon. How long were you married?"

Savannah didn't want to discuss her ex. Though she refused to utter his name, she decided to toss Jackson something for good-naturedly enduring the grilling she'd given him about Angelica. "We dated for a year, then we got married. It lasted a little less than two years."

"What happened?"

"I outgrew him."

Jackson glanced away from the road with a look that clearly conveyed he wanted to know more. "Oh?"

"I left him. Smartest thing I've ever done," Savannah replied, not to boast but to dispel any notions that there might be lingering regrets on her part.

Companionable silence ensued for the next few miles.

Jackson swung the Acura onto the highway. She counted at least a half dozen exits whizzing by the windows. "So are you going to give me a hint where we're headed?"

"To my place." Jackson appeared to be gauging her response to that bit of news.

"Oh?" Savannah lifted a brow and a smile teased her lips.

"You don't mind, do you?"

"Oh, no! I'd love to see where you live," Savannah replied too quickly. But she'd never been one of those women good at playing games for long. If she liked a man, he usually found out within the first two or three dates, which according to "The Rules" was the quickest way to turn one off. Men liked the chase, she'd been told. It was in their nature to prize that which wasn't so easily acquired. Maybe that was the real reason Jackson wasn't making a play for the bodacious Angelica, who was practically panting for him.

All Savannah knew was she had to be true to who she was. She wasn't about to play aloof or feign disinterest to reel in some guy. If he couldn't respect her for who and what she was, to hell with him, which was why she'd presented Bryce with divorce papers when he'd attempted to mold her into someone else.

"Good," Jackson broke into her thoughts. "Are you hungry?"

Savannah didn't realize she was until he asked. "Yes." She checked the clock on his dash and realized it was nearing the dinner rush, such as it was, at the Silver Spoon. She wondered if things were running smoothly, but decided not to fret about it. Troy was a whiz at taking charge and he had her cell phone number in the event of an emergency. Her baby was in capable hands.

Jackson's elegant two-story brick house sat amid a lush, well-manicured lawn, canopied by a family of robust elms. The neighborhood sat on a cusp, separating the city from the suburbs.

Jackson opened the door and let Savannah enter first. The foyer extended to an open layout with views of the living room, kitchen and formal dining room. The high ceilings added to its airy spaciousness. Overstuffed leather furniture and contemporary glass-top and wrought-iron tables semi-circled the room's focal point, an elegant black marble fireplace.

"Make yourself comfortable while I get you a drink." Jackson removed his sport jacket and stored it in the closet near the front door. "What would you like? I have wine, brandy, juice and soft drinks."

"A glass of chardonnay sounds good if you have it." Savannah sank on the butter soft sofa cushions. There were a few pieces of African art bric-a-brac she couldn't identify with certainty as she scanned the room. She took in details and attempted to decipher what everything might reveal about her host. Uncluttered, low key, yet elegant and mysterious, both the man and the room.

Smooth jazz filled the background from an unseen stereo system.

When Jackson returned and passed Savannah a glass of wine, she noticed he'd removed his shoes and rolled up the sleeves of his crisp white shirt. "Take off your shoes. Get comfortable."

Savannah took his advice and slipped out of her mules.

"You're welcome to stay out here if you want to relax and enjoy the music," he said. "But I'd love it if you'd join me in my kitchen."

"Of course, I'm curious to see where one who trained at one of the top cooking institutes in America works his magic." Sipping her wine, Savannah came to her feet and followed him, noting the power and grace in each of his steps. Exquisite muscle layered the tall frame beneath the clothing.

"Wow!" Savannah's jaw dropped when she entered the brightly lit, immaculate kitchen. "No wonder you wanted me to join you. You're obviously very proud of this kitchen!"

Jackson grinned. "I wanted your company as well."

"Yeah, right." Savannah chuckled as she took in everything the large stainless steel Sub-Zero refrigerator, Wolf range and thick, blond butcher block island and counters. A cluster of gleaming steel cookware was suspended overhead. "What? No expensive copper pots and pans?"

"For insufferable show-offs," he replied drolly.

"And this kitchen from chef's heaven is not?"

"Copper does conduct heat better and they look real snazzy and all, but they're a pain in the ass to keep clean."

Savannah completed his thought. "So what's for dinner?"

"I hope you like fish."

"I love fish any way I can get it—fried, sautéed, baked, blackened, grilled. You name it."

Savannah and Jackson bounded from one topic to another as he busied himself slicing and dicing vegetables, then seasoning their fish.

An hour later, Savannah helped Jackson prepare the dining table for their feast of salmon, asparagus and salad.

Savannah finished her last bite of her scrumptious dessert, a leftover homemade peach cobbler they had zapped in the microwave. She dabbed at her lips with a soft cloth napkin. "That was delicious, Jackson."

"Glad you liked it." Jackson had prepared two cappuccinos. He placed the cups on a small wicker tray and beckoned for Savannah to join him in the living room.

Jackson rested the tray on the coffee table.

When Savannah sat on the sofa behind it, he folded his long frame close to hers. He draped his arm along the back, letting his hand casually caress her shoulder.

Savannah had to say what had been on her mind since he'd whisked her away from that Sunbeam Girl meeting earlier that day. "You've been incredibly nice to me, between the *Aida* tickets, the superb home-cooked meal and the sweet talk. I must say you really know how to spoil a girl."

They shifted their bodies to prepare for a kiss. "A woman like you deserves to be spoiled, Savannah," Jackson said, lifting her hand to his mouth. Her name seemed to flow over the rumble of his sexy baritone. It could coax her into just about anything.

He leaned closer to cover her mouth with his own in a slow, sensual exploration that set her on fire from the inside out. The kiss intensified as he drew her closer still. She savored the feel of her breasts crushing against the unyielding hardness of chest. Her hands massaged the nape of his neck. Savannah had to feel and taste more of him. She nibbled at the flesh on his neck. Her hands stole to free the buttons of his shirt and push away fabric. She stroked the velvety steel of his full, chiseled pecs.

Jackson cupped her bottom and in a swift maneuver positioned her to straddle his lap.

Her breath caught when she felt his formidable erection against her pubic bone, thrilling her enough to shove discretion to the recesses of her mind. It had been too long since she'd enjoyed this type of intimacy. She'd never been with a man on the first date. And normally their time together would've had to unfold exceptionally well for him to get an open-mouth kiss after a few weeks. What she was considering right now was completely out of character. But she sensed there would be much more between her and Jackson than the physical. Sex would be just one of many spectacular aspects of what was to come, she told herself.

Jackson pushed her dress up and squeezed her bottom, pressing her closer to him. Need coursed through her veins and throbbed at her center. She rubbed herself against him and savored the sweet friction. The kiss deepened to a mingling of souls.

Savannah tore her lips away just long enough to moan. "Oh, Jackson, I just know you're going to feel so good."

"And I want to make you feel good." Jackson softly suckled the skin on her neck. He moved one hand from her rear and let his fingers flutter at the moist silky fabric at the cove between her thighs, nudging her toward an exquisite madness as she ground against him.

"Jackson," she managed through thick, ragged breaths. She wanted him inside her when she edged toward the precipice of complete satisfaction. "Um…do you have protection?"

For a moment, Savannah thought she felt the rest of his body go stiff, as the erection wedged between them went soft.

His fingers halted their expert machinations. As if he'd been slapped, air gushed out of his lungs. Clumsy silence stretched between them as Savannah studied his face. His smooth forehead pleated. She pressed her hand against his angular jaw. "Jackson, are you all right?" she asked. He averted his gaze, but she angled his face to search his eyes. "Is everything all right?"

Jackson answered by drawing her close, in a protective hug. But the passionate moment was lost.

"What just happened here?" she asked again.

Jackson gently maneuvered her until she had no choice but to move from his lap.

He came to his feet, dragging a hand through his short curls. "I'm sorry, Savannah. I—I didn't mean to get carried away like that. This is our first official date…"

Savannah went to him and curled her arms around his lean waist. "But it's okay, Jackson. Really it is. I-I want you."

Jackson moved away, buttoning his shirt. "It's getting late. I'd better get you home."

Not the response Savannah expected. His gaze flitted everywhere but on her. The tone of his voice remained warm and even, but it was as if some invisible wall had slammed down between them. She wasn't into playing games, but she also wasn't so hard up for male attention that she'd beg him to take what she was willing to offer. "Fine," she said, forcing a casual note into her reply and adjusting her disheveled clothing. "You can take me to the Silver Spoon. It's just about closing time."

Jackson reached for his keys on the coffee table and led the way to the door.

CHAPTER 7

Vince's date with Angie couldn't have played better if he'd scripted and directed it himself. Now it appeared as if the evening would finally end with a bang—literally.

After the photo shoot he and Angie went their separate ways, but made plans to get together for dinner at Cesaro's and of all things—the damn opera. The opera. Vince had to make sure the other fellas in the photography department wouldn't get wind of that or he'd never hear the end of it.

Vince had scored the tickets because of an award-winning photo essay of the opera house for one of those glossy architectural magazines three years ago. Since then the opera house director had made it a point to mail Vince complimentary tickets of select productions. Vince, who would rather kick back with a cold brew at a Reds game or Wrestlemania, usually passed his opera tickets to that nice little old lady named Abigail, who worked at the *Tribune*'s receptionist desk. He hadn't gotten around to ditching the *La Traviata* tickets that had arrived two days earlier and when he'd casually mentioned he still had them,

Angie appeared to regard him with a newfound appreciation.

It was all Vince could do to keep from keeling over five minutes into all that singing that sounded like a chorus of drunken cats. Glass-shattering soprano notes hurt his ears, which was why he'd never really gotten into Mariah "Dog Whistle" Carey either.

But the eardrum abuse he'd suffered at *La Traviata* had been worth it when Angie invited him back to her place for a drink. It was all so perfect.

Angie had proven to be even hotter than he had hoped. She had been flirting up a storm all evening. And she'd made a point to dress for a private celebration, done up like a Christmas present just waiting to be unwrapped. Tight, revealing clothing with little ties, bows, snaps, straps, strings and things often screamed "undo me and do me!" Vince's fingers itched to release the ties of her halter-styled dress. Angelica led him down a concrete walkway and stopped at the front door of her brick duplex. "Thanks again for inviting me to the show. It was wonderful," she said as she searched for her keys inside a small clutch bag.

"Good. I'm glad you enjoyed yourself." At least one of them had, Vince decided. During the show the thigh-high slit and the low scoop neck of her electric blue dress were the only things that had kept him awake. When he hadn't been fantasizing about palming Angie's ripe breasts and butt, he was wondering how her lips would taste.

Angie opened the door, switched on the lights. "Bet that threw you for a loop, huh?"

"What threw me for a loop?"

"The fact that I actually liked the show. Come out with it. Few people suspect that I have *La Bohème* and *Falstaff* stashed among my Da Brat, DMX, and Bone Thugs-N-Harmony CDs. But I'll let you in on a little secret. I actually enjoy *NSYNC, too."

"You mean *NStink, don't you?" He laughed. "Such eclectic musical taste."

"Yeah, eclectic. That's me." Angie reached for Vince's jacket. "Here, let me put that away. Take a load off." She gestured toward an overstuffed sofa in her living room.

Vince strode over and strategically settled on the middle cushion. He'd have easy access to her regardless of which cushion she chose. He loosened his tie and relaxed.

He heard Angie puttering around the kitchen preparing their drinks. "So how long have you been an opera aficionado?"

"I never said I was an aficionado." Angie glanced at him from the kitchen. "I just enjoy listening to the music every now and then. There's something so deeply emotional about it. It's weird because I can't speak a lick of Italian. But opera is the kind of music that breaks down language barriers and touches my soul—almost as deeply as gospel. Know what I mean?"

He didn't, but he nodded anyway. "So when were you first bitten by the opera bug?" He kept this thread of conversation going to show that he was interested in whatever interested her tonight.

"Tenth grade, but the credit goes to Mrs. Beatrice Calloway, my music teacher."

"Really a teacher, huh?"

"Yup. And she made quite an impression on me, too. Before Mrs. Calloway I thought opera was just for the country club types who had trust funds and names like Muffy and Biff. Mrs. Calloway was the hippest teacher at George Washington Carver High School. Anyway, I experienced my first opera on a class field trip that Mrs. Calloway arranged. I remember it as if it were yesterday. I saw my first live stage production of Mozart's *Così fan tutte*. At first I was too put off by the Italian and the subtitles they projected above the stage kinda worked my nerves. That's why I never liked foreign flicks. Subtitles!" She made a face. "But anyway, before I knew it I was sucked into the story. All that double dating, double crossing and double identity stuff was just as juicy as anything I'd seen on *The Young and the Restless*." Angelica had two glasses. She joined Vince on the sofa. "Ready to wet your whistle with my best cognac?"

"I can hardly wait," Vince drawled with a knowing grin. He took a sip of cognac, sure she was about to make her move.

"So. Here we are. I've been wanting to ask you something all night."

"Shoot." Vince let his hand curl around her soft, bare shoulder.

"What's the real story behind why you've been bugging me to go out with you all these weeks?"

"Why wouldn't I ask you out?" he pitched the question back. "You're a very beautiful woman, Angie, I mean Angelica. I'm sure men ask you out all the time. From the moment I laid eyes on you I hoped you weren't attached because I wanted to get to know you better."

"Really?"

Vince tried on a meek smile, which he hoped revealed nothing of what he was really thinking. Yes, he wanted to know Angelica better, but more importantly he wanted to see her buck naked, glistening in sweat after a marathon session of teeth-rattling sex, but not necessarily in that order. It wasn't just Angie's God-given assets, but her provocative, in-your-face style that intrigued the hell out of Vince. What man could miss the sprayed-on minis, low-cut tops, spike-heeled shoes she favored? This was obviously a woman who was proud of her body and more than happy to show it off. He just hoped her predilection for displaying the goodies extended to a willingness to share them. He wasn't up to jumping through a bunch of dating ritual hoops. He wanted instant gratification. No strings attached.

Vince's world was not one controlled by proper appearances, rigid rules, suffocating regimen or long-term relationships. At least not anymore. He wasn't about to set himself up for a fall again. As long as he focused on the physical side of the dating game, lines weren't blurred, things stayed simple. And most importantly, feelings—his in particular—did not get hurt.

Vince pulled Angie closer. He'd been dying to taste her lips and press her honey-dipped body close to his. She responded as he'd hoped she would, eagerly opening to him. He caressed her silky thighs and kissed her as if he could just gobble her up whole. He instantly grew hot and hard. He reached for the zipper of his pants, then patted his pockets to check for his triple-packet of Trojans. She suddenly went stiff in his arms and pulled away from their kiss.

"Something wrong?" he asked, through short, ragged breaths.

Angie searched his eyes, then quickly shook her head. "N—No."

But he'd noticed a change in her expression as if a veil of disappointment now shadowed her pretty features. Nah, he was probably imagining it, he decided, pushing the thought to the back of his mind as he moved in for the kill, closing the distance between them again with another breath-stifling kiss. He patted his pockets again, thinking he'd underestimated how many rubbers he'd need, but he wouldn't sweat it. He was sure Angie had her own stash.

She pulled away again. "I'm going to slip into something more comfortable," Angie cooed as she gently pried her lips away from his. "You do the same. Get comfortable, I mean." She nipped his bottom lip with her teeth and released a wicked little growl before detangling her limbs from his.

Grinning, Vince ogled her bubble-shaped rump as she departed. Angie peered over her shoulder and winked at him, then disappeared inside her bedroom. Once the door was sealed, he discarded his shoes, socks and pants as if they were on fire. Luther Vandross's velvety vocals wafted from her bedroom. Vince debated whether to doff his purple silk briefs, then decided to leave a little something for Angie to remove.

He tried to get comfortable on the sofa, but that was tricky with a boner standing as tall and unyielding as Mount Everest. The slip of light beneath Angie's bedroom door dimmed to a muted glow. He watched, waited and salivated.

Then waited some more. He checked the star-shaped art deco clock on the wall. She'd been in there at least a good twenty minutes. What was taking her so long?

"Oh, Angie, I mean An-ge-li-ca," Vince crooned.

A melancholy Luther warbled.

Vince got up and moved just outside the bedroom door. "Oh, An-ge-li-ca," he sang again. No response, just more of Luther's silky soul vocals.

He tapped on the door twice and waited for an invitation. He tapped again, then slowly cracked the door. "Angelica." He stepped inside. The sensual scent of patchouli from at least a dozen lighted candles filled the room. The four-poster bed was empty, but a pair of handcuffs and a whip hung from the two posts at the head of the bed. Damn! This babe was kinkier than he'd thought. Vince smiled, rubbing his hands together in delight. The satin blue push-up bra that Angie had worn earlier was the first garment he noticed on the floor. "Angelica, come out, come out wherever you are," he sang, following the alluring clothing trail. He stepped over her dress, the garter belt and stockings Angie had peeled off. The sliding glass and screen door in the bedroom were open. Vertical blinds were drawn to one side. Silk curtains stretched along a night breeze. Vince noticed what appeared to be a pair of black panties on the deck. He stepped outside for a closer inspection. If she wanted to do it in the great outdoors, he was certainly down with that. He hadn't done the do under the moon and the stars in a long, long time. He slid his fingers along the glass surface of a large circular patio table. He deemed it sturdy enough to withstand the force of the most athletic fun and games. The backyard stretched out a couple of acres to an L-shaped strip of trees. Angelica's place was half of a duplex, which broke the illusion of complete privacy. Not a problem, though. A small partition and fence sliced the patio and the yard into equal parts. Besides, the possibility of getting caught was part of the thrill of outdoor sex.

"Angelica," Vince called out again as he scooped up the satin panties that had no crotch. Oooohh-la-la! He was sure Angie hadn't been wearing these earlier. Maybe she'd model them now. Vince heard the screen door behind him swoosh closed.

"There you are," he said smoothly as he turned. If this was some sort of newfangled way she got her groove on, he didn't want to appear to be out of the loop. As he reached for the screen's handle, he noticed that Angie was fully clothed in an old Dallas Cowboys sweatshirt and a pair of over-sized, faded Levis. The door wouldn't budge. "I think it's stuck. Can you help me out here?"

"It's not stuck." Angie's frosty tone and the cold glint in her eyes sent shivers over his skin though the temperature hovered somewhere in the mid-eighties. "It's locked."

"Open it up, then." Vince jiggled it roughly with no success.

Angie pursed her red lips into a tight little knot, much smaller than the one suddenly forming in Vince's stomach.

"What are you up to?" Vince chuckled, trying to hide the mounting anxiety of being on the wrong side of the screen door in his underwear.

Angelica wrinkled her nose as if she smelled something foul. "What do you think I'm up to?"

"Oh, I get it. You're into little hide-and-seek games as foreplay, eh?" Vince jiggled the handle some more. "That's cool. I can dig it."

"Yup. But this game is called 'How to Get Even With A First Date Who Tries to Play You Like A Stank Two-Dollar Skank.' Ever heard of that one?"

"What?" Vince questioned whether he'd heard her right. "You were leading me on all night like you wanted something to happen."

"Tell me one thing, just one thing, I did or said tonight that could be reasonably construed as an invitation to my boudoir," she demanded as she latched one hand on her hip.

"What about when you…There was that thing you said about…" Vince searched his memory, but couldn't think of anything more conclusive than his own wishful thinking. Had he misread her signals? Had she even sent any signals? "You invited me back to your place."

"For a drink and some conversation. Nothing more. I was still trying to give you the benefit of the doubt. I kept hoping you'd redeem yourself. I really wanted this to work out."

"But that kiss on your sofa?"

"It was supposed to be a kiss, Vince. A K-I-S-S. And every woman you kiss automatically falls into bed with you? You were reaching for your zipper and doing your little condom check as soon as you slipped your tongue in my mouth. And you thought you were so smooth. I've seen horny ninth graders with slicker moves."

"What about the candles? Luther? The crotchless panties?"

"As fast as you were moving, I had a feeling you wouldn't waste any time jumping out of your clothes. That stuff was all part of the set-up to get you right where I wanted you, out there…in a compromising position, of course," she gloated.

Vince pitched the panties he didn't realize he was still clutching to the ground and swatted at the mosquitoes that began feasting on him. "And the handcuffs? The whip? So you just happened to have those things lying around."

"Props left over from the male stripper and the bachelorette party I hosted for a close friend a few months ago. I kept them around for laughs, but looks as if the joke's on you." Angie let her gaze drop to his briefs then brought it back up again. "For the record, while I'm nobody's prude, when I do decide to let things get more intimate, I like to get to know a man first, establish a foundation and genuine feelings based on something more substantial than the urge to merge. Sure I can work the vamp thing, but I'm not— I repeat—I'm not an easy lay, Lomax. And I don't know where you got that idea."

Running out of patience, Vince was poised to strike below the belt. "Maybe it was just the powerful hoochie vibes you were sending out to Jackson and those come-and-get-it clothes you wear to work. Care to explain those?"

Angie glared, her jaw working as she gritted her teeth and folded her arms under her breasts. "So I like sexy clothes. What of it?"

"Sexy clothes? You mean scandalous clothes. You make Lil' Kim look like the damn Church Lady."

"Since when did a sexy dress become a sign language for 'bed me?'"

"Since the dating game became all about the hunter and the hunted," Vince pointed out. "Men are programmed to chase and women are programmed to make their bait as enticing as possible. I'm sure you spent quite a bit of time fussing over what to wear tonight. You chose that dress because you wanted to send a simple, singular message. You want men to want you, desire you, lust after you. You won. Hey, I'm a proud owner of a Y chromosome. I'm hot— burning up—for you. So what's the problem?"

"But is it my body or my brain, Vince?"

"It wasn't your brain spilling out of that tight dress tonight, darlin'," Vince retorted. Then he gave a belabored sigh and added, "Okay, Angelica, so you've made your point. Obviously, there isn't going to be any bones jumping tonight. Now let me in."

"No," she replied like a spoiled child refusing to go beddy-bye.

"You're not letting me back in?" She'd already made it clear that she wasn't ever going to crawl between the sheets with Vince, much to his dismay. What more did she want?

"Not until you apologize and promise to treat all women with more respect instead of blow-up dolls who merely exist for your personal pleasure." Angie leaned on the door's frame. "I enjoyed some of your conversation tonight, but then you had to go and blow it with all the sexual innuendo and raunchy double entendre that you thought was so clever and amusing. And that thing you did with that crab leg and the raspberry pastry…" She winced as her words dropped off. "Totally juvenile and crass—especially when I was trying to eat. Treat ladies like ladies!"

"I will…when I see one." Vince regretted the barb the moment it jumped off his lips.

Angie flinched before her expression gave way to anger. "Oh yeah? Well, since you're so hot to trot, I have the perfect way to cool you down."

Angie disappeared, but a few seconds later he heard the spurt and swish of the yard sprinklers. Tall streams formed a wide water fan. Vince pounded on the screen door, shouting as the water sprayed over him, "Angelica! Open this goddamn door! Now!"

His briefs were soaked and he felt their cargo shrink faster than a cheap acrylic sock in the wrong dry cycle. Vince hadn't been so humiliated since he was ten years old when his cousin Cordell had practically yanked Vince's new Aqua Man swimming trunks up to his chin. That super turbo atomic wedgie had made him the laughingstock among all the kids at his pool party.

Angie returned. "Go ahead, yell your head off. That'll get nosy ol' Mrs. Dinglebaum's attention all right. She lives on the other side of this duplex. She sleeps light and she has the hearing of a canine. She'll think you're some sort of pervert prowler and call 911," she taunted him. "When they show up I'll be sure to tell them I've never seen you before in my life and that you must've gotten my name off my mailbox. Wonder who they'll believe? Me or some crazy dude running around outdoors in wet, mauve-colored underwear?"

"My briefs aren't mauve! They're purple!"

"Whatever," Angie flapped a hand breezily.

"When I get my hands on you, I'm going to wring your neck," Vince ground out.

"Tsk! Tsk!" Angelica's sweet smile belied the evil gleam in eyes. "Threats will get you nowhere," she chirped.

The light came on next door. The raspy voice of an old woman called out, "Who's there? Anybody out there?"

"Shit!" Vince hissed under his breath.

"That would be ol' Mrs. Dinglebaum," Angie informed him as she proceeded to slowly close the glass patio door, erecting an additional shield between them.

"Wait!" The word rushed out like strong gust of wind. "I'm sorry I treated you like...like...less than the lady that you obviously are. I promise to be mindful of how I treat all women in the future—regardless of how short and tight their skirts are."

Angie paused, picked at her nails, seemingly captivated by her own cuticles. "Hmmmm. Well…" She was obviously evaluating the sincerity of his apology. "I question whether you've really learned your lesson. I'm not a fan of negative reinforcement, but—"

"But I did exactly as you asked. What more do you want from me? I made a mistake, misjudged the situation and misread your signals. Okay? Cut me some slack," Vince demanded.

"I know somebody is out there. I'm calling the cops, you hear," Mrs. Dinglebaum threatened, her voice hitching a few octaves.

Vince crouched to hide beneath the patio table.

"It's okay, Mrs. Dinglebaum," Angie finally called out, chuckling. "It's just me, Angelica, and a…um…uh…friend clowning around."

"Okay dear, just checking," Mrs. Dinglebaum replied. "Can't be too careful."

The old woman's light went off and the sprinklers followed. Vince thanked Angie, begrudgingly.

"Go stand in the middle of the yard and turn around after you've slowly counted to ten," Angie instructed him.

Vince stood to his full height. "What for? So you can resume drowning me?"

"My mama didn't raise a fool. I'm not taking any chances on you retaliating tonight. I'm going to put your clothes and keys out here on the patio so you can get dressed. Then I want you to get the hell off my property."

Vince made up his mind to swallow all smarmy retorts until he had his keys and clothes securely in hand. He did as she asked and stood in the middle of the lawn, then counted to ten. He heard the screen door slide open. He turned in time to see Angie shoving his belongings and a large fluffy towel out on the deck.

Vince muttered as he dried his skin with the towel. He quickly slipped on his slacks, which sopped up the moisture from his briefs like a cloth diaper.

"And to think, I thought I saw glimpses of your charming side today, when you pretended to care about my feelings. Must've been a mirage," Angie snorted with a tinge of sadness. "I'm disappointed because I was close to actually giving you the benefit of the doubt. I guess it just wasn't meant to be. Ciao." She sealed the glass door and clicked the lock.

CHAPTER 8

Jackson usually looked forward to spring and Sundays at Julian's. After church services, he'd follow his twin to his sprawling suburban home. The two would kick back with a six pack, shoot the breeze and enjoy the view of a perfect, sparkling day from his cedar deck out back.

They'd watch Sasha and her best buddies from the neighborhood splash around in their huge aboveground swimming pool. Soon they'd get a signal from Julian's wife, Darlene, that a mouth-watering meal was about to be served.

Today Julian flitted from one topic to the next and Jackson found it too difficult to keep up his end of the conversation. That scene of Savannah and himself on his couch the night before played in his head in a nonstop loop.

Julian's voice faded out and all he could hear was Savannah's passionate whisper: "Oh, Jackson, I just know you're going to feel so good."

An alarming realization had swept over him. He obviously wasn't as ready as he'd hoped. But would he ever be again?

"Hey, you!" Julian reached over and slapped Jackson's arm. "Where did you go just now?"

Jolted from his reverie, Jackson's legs straddled his deck chair.

"What's up with you?" Julian asked. "You've looked out of it all day."

"I'm fine." Jackson brushed off the inquiry, averting his gaze.

"Look, it's me, man. You know we can't fake each other like that. You know how you always know when something's off with me. Well, you know I have the same spooky twin's sixth sense going, so just go on and spill it now."

Jackson would have to put his pride aside and talk to someone. If he couldn't trust his twin brother with something so sensitive, who could he trust?

Jackson took a swig of beer from his can and dove in. "It's that procedure I had a few months ago—"

Julian, who'd been slumping in his deck chair, sat upright. "You didn't get bad news at your last checkup, did you?"

"No, it's nothing like that. Doc actually gave me a clean bill of health, physically at least," Jackson replied as he watched Sasha hurl herself off the end of a diving board to break the surface of the water with a cannonball splash. Two of her pals followed close behind, squealing in delight.

"Hey, Jabari!" Julian shouted at a chubby boy in blue swim trunks, who had lassoed himself a sunburned little blonde. "Stop horsing around with that jump rope before somebody gets hurt."

The boy mumbled something, but resumed his antics.

"Hey, don't make me come over there!" Julian warned just before the boy freed the bucking girl. Satisfied, he turned his attention back to his brother. "So what's the problem, man?"

Jackson closed his eyes and pinched the bridge of his nose where tension pulsed. "I don't know."

"I met this…" He sucked in a deep breath. "This beautiful, fascinating woman three weeks ago."

"That Savannah. Yeah, I remember you told me about her. She sounds nice."

"We went to a show and I took her back to my place for a nice romantic dinner."

"She must be pretty special if you're cooking for her already."

"Yes, she is. Things were moving along great, too. The lights were low. The music was as smooth as the wine. I had her in my arms. The vibe was so perfect. She was diggin' me as much as I was diggin' her. We both wanted each other something fierce. There was nothing holding either of us back until… until…" Jackson faltered.

Julian shoved Jackson's shoulder. "Until what? You can't leave me hanging like that."

Jackson quaffed his beer, hoping a good buzz would help him get it out. "I choked, man. I totally choked."

"What do you mean, you 'choked'? You didn't close?" Julian asked a little too loudly for Jackson's comfort.

"Sshhhhh!" Jackson flapped both hands at Julian

"Darlene's in the kitchen and the kids are squealing so loud I can barely hear myself think," Julian pointed out.

"No, I didn't close," Jackson said in a stage whisper. "The sail came up, but I didn't get the ship anywhere near the harbor, if you catch my drift. I panicked then lost my…well, you know."

"Oh, was there some pain or discomfort? It's been like…what? Like six or seven months since that prostate surgery, right?"

"Yeah, seven months."

"But you were given a clean bill of health, right?"

"Yeah, save for some slight residual swelling that I have a prescription for, everything checks out."

"So the problem is mental, not physical?"

Jackson nodded. "Must be. As I said, the plumbing seems to be in working order, but once Savannah started moaning about how gooooood she just knew it would feel…something inside my head snapped and I freaked."

"Performance anxiety?"

"Struck big time, out of the blue, it seems."

"So she's your first since you had the surgery?"

"Yes. And she's the first woman that's awakened the sleeping bear, if you know what I mean."

His brother's brows hitched about a mile. "Really? Been that long, huh?"

"Don't look so surprised."

"It's just that...well...I hate to admit this," Julian tried to smother a grin, "but between the two of us, you were always the simmering sex machine. Man, before your surgery, you needed to store your little black books using the Dewey Decimal system."

"Don't remind me, but I've turned over a new leaf. I'm not just looking for a playmate, but a soul mate."

"So let me get this straight. So you did...um...respond to the woman, right? That's a good sign. Everything should be fine. What are you worried about?"

Jackson took another thirsty gulp of his beer. "Disappointing her, being a little too quick on the draw."

Julian shot him an incredulous look. "This from the one Beverly Winfrow once dubbed 'Stamina Man?'"

Surprised, Jackson felt his face flush. "Hey, how did you know about that old nickname?"

Julian chuckled. "Seems the fairer sex can blab, too. We have the locker room and the ladies have the powder room. You forget Bev and my old girl Joselyn were tight."

"Jeez." Jackson shook his head in disbelief. "They were discussing—"

"Don't even try to act as if you're bent out of shape. You've given me the blow-by-blow enough times."

"Yeah, but you're my brother and I haven't given you a 'blow-by-blow,' as you call it, on any lady I've been involved with since college. We've both outgrown that sort of bravado about our sexual exploits."

"True, but what I think you're trying to tell me is you're feeling the pressure of living up that old 'Stamina Man' label."

Jackson looked out into the distance, quietly considering his brother's observation.

"Look, you just met this Savannah. You two sound as if you're very hot for each other, but where is it written that you have to act on it right now? Savor this time, when it's all so fresh, new and exciting. There's nothing like the first rush of romance. Draw out the anticipation. And there's certainly nothing wrong with getting to know each other better."

"Funny, that's not what you said when you first met Darlene. You were all over that woman the first week."

"Yeah, but Darlene made me wait and had me so crazy after awhile if she'd tossed me a bone, I would've caught it between my teeth."

Jackson chuckled at the mental image of Julian fetching like Fido.

"Just chill, give yourself some time. And when the time is right, everything will fall into place." Julian reached over and patted his brother's shoulder.

"You think?" Jackson asked, loathing the fear and hollow uncertainty in his own voice.

Sundays at the Silver Spoon were usually slow, so the half-full dining room was reason to celebrate. But Savannah couldn't stop berating herself long enough to work up the enthusiasm.

She moved about the dining room with a plastered-on smile, greeting patrons and inquiring whether there was anything she could do to make their dining experience more enjoyable. She'd passed along Jackson's advice and her serving staff had increased its efficiency. There was a short wait time between orders placed and food delivered. And fewer ordering screw-ups. Between tables Savannah's thoughts circled back to the previous night at Jackson's house.

What must the man think after she'd practically thrown herself at him? And on their first official date, no less. No wonder he'd pushed her away. If she was so willing to give herself to him so quickly, what was to prevent him from thinking she'd made a practice of such premature sexual dalliances with others? She'd tried on a new sexual attitude for size, but now she felt the pinch of regret. She was a grown woman, for crying out loud, and last night she'd wanted Jackson so bad she could still feel the lingering ache of having to part unfulfilled. Get a grip! Still uncertain whether he'd ever call her again, she'd clung to the hope that she hadn't completely turned him off with her over-aggressiveness. Then she inwardly upbraided herself for caring so much so soon. She was supposed to be a carefree, modern, single woman, right? They weren't teenagers caught steaming up car windows at a drive-in. And he hadn't been an unwilling participant up until the moment he'd frozen up on her in mid-kiss. If his intentions had been completely wholesome, would his hands have been up her skirt and between her legs so quickly?

"Savannah." The voice of her newest waitress startled her. "Eloise is in the back waiting for you."

"Thanks, Clara. So, how's the family?" Savannah asked.

"Everyone's fine, ma'am," Clara replied with a smile.

"Good. Glad to hear it." Before moving toward the kitchen, Savannah noted that the woman's gaunt cheeks had already begun to appear rosier and plumped out, the result of having better access to more balanced meals. That made her smile. Giving the woman a break had been a great idea.

Inside the kitchen Savannah found Eloise teaching Percy and Emma Jean how to handle garlic. The two assistant cooks gave the older woman their undivided attention.

"Isn't a garlic press more efficient?" Emma Jean asked.

"No, it will compromise the flavor. Always take the time to cut garlic in tiny little slivers." Eloise demonstrated with an inch-long clove using a paring knife and a cutting board. "Just like this. See?" When she'd completed the task, Eloise looked up. "Oh hello, Savannah honey."

"So how are your two star pupils doing?" Savannah used a clean fork to pluck a slice of fresh cucumber from the heap piled in one of the large bowls on the counter.

"Percy and Emma Jean are quick studies. They're doing great."

"It's not as if we're starting from scratch, you know." Percy, a wiry fifty-something man whose crabby demeanor failed to mask his soft heart, said, "I was a cook before I came to work here, you know."

Percy's cooking experience had been limited to hole-in-the-wall greasy spoons and Emma Jean had been a cook at one of the cheesy chain joints—Bake & Broast Bird. Savannah had hired the two not because of their impressive restaurant credentials, but because they'd been close friends of Fannie Cooper, the woman who had taken her and Troy in those last four years they were in the foster care system. Fannie had passed away six years ago, but

Savannah believed providing better employment opportunities for Emma Jean and Percy was a way to honor her foster mother's memory.

Before Felix quit, Savannah had hoped the more experienced head chef could fill in the gaps in Emma Jean and Percy's culinary training. Fortunately, Eloise's expertise did extend beyond desserts and she'd happily agreed to take on the temporary role of head chef until a suitable permanent replacement could be found.

"Eloise, do you have a minute?" Savannah asked as she opened the door leading to her office.

"Sure. Just give me a second, all right?" Eloise turned back to Emma Jean and Percy. "Remember, the vinaigrette takes one teaspoon of finely diced ginger, two tablespoons of finely diced shallots and what else?"

"One tablespoon of sherry vinegar, one tablespoon of canola," Emma Jean added proudly.

"Percy?" Eloise prodded, waving her paring knife like a ruler-wielding schoolmarm.

Percy released an exasperated breath, then rolled his eyes skyward before replying, "One tablespoon of soy, a half teaspoon of fresh lime juice and um…um…"

"A pinch of cayenne!" Emma Jean added.

"So Emma Jean gets the gold star for today," Percy remarked sourly.

Eloise beamed. "You both get gold stars! Now, I'm going to go chat with Savannah. I'll be right back."

Daphne entered the kitchen with more orders. Business seemed to be picking up as the evening wore on.

Wiping her hands on the bib apron tied around her thick torso, Eloise took the seat across from Savannah's desk.

"I just want to thank you again for agreeing to help me out," Savannah said. "You can see from our growing clientele and return business that your presence has made a big impact on the Silver Spoon."

"Thank you, honey. I wanted to offer my help sooner, but I didn't want to seem too pushy. After all, it was awfully nice of you to carry my desserts in your restaurant. I didn't want to come on too strong by giving you unsolicited advice on the rest of your menu. I'm so flattered that you thought enough of my skills to ask for my input."

"Well, actually, I can't take all the credit for the idea. A friend..." Savannah searched for the appropriate label for Jackson. "I mean, um...a restaurant consultant who tasted your desserts advised me to recruit you, and Troy seconded the suggestion. I'm glad I listened." She used a key to open a side desk drawer, removed an envelope and passed it to Eloise.

"What this?" the older woman asked.

"Look inside." Savannah smiled.

Eloise's hand flew to her mouth when she saw the crisp bills inside. "But you've already paid me the price we agreed upon for my help."

"I know, but you've done such a bang-up job on revamping the menu and working with Emma Jean and Percy. I thought you deserved a little bonus. Shoot, dealing with Percy's curmudgeonly attitude alone is worth the extra cash. I know he's a softie on the inside, but that sourpuss exterior can grate a bit if you're not used to him."

Savannah joined Eloise in her laughter until Troy interrupted them. "Savannah, Jackson's out front."

"He is?" Savannah's heart did a flip-flop.

Eloise's eyes sparkled with interest. "Hmmm. From the way your face lit up just now, I'd venture to guess that's your fella, huh?"

"He's a…um…friend," Savannah replied with an air of mystery.

"Oh?" Eloise was not convinced. "Is that what they're calling them these days?"

Savannah had forgotten Eloise occasionally displayed a tendency to stick her nose where it didn't belong, but the woman had worked such wonders in one short week that Savannah would have gladly taken the time to indulge her curiosity if Jackson weren't waiting. She reached inside a bottom drawer and removed a compact. She checked her hair and applied a fresh coat of lipstick.

Mercifully, Eloise took the hint and moved toward the door. "I'd better get back out there and check on that vinaigrette dressing. And you don't want to keep your fella..." she pointedly cleared her throat, "I mean, your friend, waiting."

Savannah spotted Jackson waiting at one of the tables near the front of the dining room. It always seemed to take time to adjust to the man's exceptional good looks and virile magnetism. She tried to look her fill and steady her racing heart when he caught a glimpse of her. He rose, slightly hovering over his seat as she approached him. He didn't take his seat again until she'd settled on hers.

"I'm so glad you came out to see me," Jackson said, wrapping his long fingers around a glass of ice water.

"Why wouldn't I?"

Jackson anxiously glanced around as if to check for eavesdroppers.

"I wasn't so sure after yesterday."

"I had a wonderful time. *Aida* was spectacular, the dinner splendid and the company..."

"I'm sure you're confused. I sent you mixed messages. I mean, what happened after dinner..."

Daphne appeared with her order pad. "Would you like something, Jackson?"

"No, I'm fine, thank you."

Daphne moved along to check on diners, then Troy seated a party of three attractive young women at the table adjacent to Savannah and Jackson's.

"You were saying?" Savannah prodded.

"Can we talk outside?" Jackson pushed his chair away from the table.

Privacy inside the Silver Spoon was hard to come by that night. For Savannah that was definitely a good thing. "Sure," she said, letting Jackson guide her out the door with a hand resting at the small of her back. "Troy, I'll be right outside if you need me."

Once outdoors, Jackson kept moving toward his Acura in the Silver Spoon parking lot. After what had happened on his couch the night before, Savannah thought it best to refrain from making a joke about necking in the back seat.

"So, here we are." Savannah tried relaxing on the passenger side as she gave Jackson a curious look.

"Yes, here we are...all alone again. Savannah, about last night..." He scooted as close as the console between them would allow and curled an arm around her shoulder. "When things heated up and I withdrew... I want you to know that had absolutely nothing to do with you." He traced an index finger softly along her cheek.

"Is there something you forgot to tell me? Is there someone else?" Her muscles stiffened as she awaited his reply.

Jackson shook his head. "Oh no, no. It's nothing like that."

"What then?" She angled her body to look him in the eye.

"You're too special to rush," he said softly, tracing her lips with the pad of one finger.

Savannah couldn't believe her ears. That was the first time she'd heard that one and it chafed a bit. She realized that wound inside of her left by her ex-husband's refusal to make love to her after she'd gained weight had yet to heal. She also couldn't help wondering if Jackson had experienced the same disgust when he'd filled his hands with thighs, butt and a waistline that had grown fluffier with the extra flesh. "You sure that's all there was to it?" The skeptical note rang clear.

"Yes, I swear. Why do you sound as if you're unsure whether to believe me or not?"

Savannah looked down at her hands resting in her lap and her voice went low. "Because...well," she hesitated. "My ex had a problem with my weight and after a while, he just came out and told me he couldn't make love to me until I went back to my former size two."

"Size two?" Jackson echoed as if he thought her ex's expectations were absurd. "I leave the dolls to my niece Sasha and her Sunbeam Girl troop. I'm a grown man and I prefer filling these big, hard hands of mine with the soft, full curves of a real woman. A lush, ripe woman I can hold and handle without fearing she might break under me if..."

Savannah looked up at him through her lashes. "If what?"

He gave her a sly grin. "If things get vigorous."

"Vigorous, you say?" A small smile tilted her lips. "So you don't have a problem with my—"

"Curves," Jackson finished her sentence. "Bryce Martin was a fool to try to give you a complex about your body. You're perfect exactly the way you are."

Jackson had leaned to close the space between them with a kiss when Savannah suddenly braced her hand against his chest and stopped him mid-pucker. "Wait. What did you just say?"

"I said you're perfect exactly the way are. Your ex was a fool." Jackson tried to complete the kiss again, but Savannah pushed away.

"You said 'Bryce Martin was a fool.'" Savannah glared at him. "How did you know I was married to Bryce Martin?"

Jackson blinked, then shrugged. "I…um…I guess you must have told me."

"Wrong answer. Try again." Savannah folded her arms across her chest and pressed her back against the door as she waited for Jackson to worm his way out of his quandary. "I made a point not to say Bryce's name because I didn't want the ghost of him hovering over us. And I made a point to tell my brother and my staff not to go spewing my personal business. So tell me, how did you know I was married to him?"

Jackson slumped back against his seat, propping his head against the rest. When he finally sat upright again, he dragged a hand down his face as his thoughts slowly emerged. "Look, Savannah. I was going to explain, but somehow, in the past three weeks the time was never quite right."

"I'm all ears," she said with an angry edge.

"Bryce has connections at the *Tribune*."

"Did those connections have anything to do with that review that appeared in the newspaper?"

Jackson nodded. "Yes. The assignment for me to review your restaurant came from Bryce's connection, but I didn't know all this until after I'd visited your restaurant and had written my review."

"So you were just an unwitting accomplice?"

"I wasn't an accomplice." He slapped the steering wheel. "I wrote that review in good conscience without being influenced by Bryce or his connection at the *Tribune*. I only found out later that Bryce had launched a crusade against the Silver Spoon and I felt bad about the role I inadvertently played in his scheme."

"If your part was as innocent as you claim, why didn't you tell me sooner?" Savannah was having trouble assimilating what Jackson was trying to tell her.

She still had too many questions and insecurities dueling inside of her. She didn't know what to believe. Suspicion and mistrust threatened to suffocate her. What if Jackson was lying and doing Bryce's dirty work? What if he'd only come up with his cock-and-bull story to cover his ass because he'd slipped and incriminated himself? What if he was still Bryce's mole, sent to insinuate himself into her life to sabotage her efforts with the Silver Spoon? What if that was the reason he'd put the brakes on what had almost happened on his sofa last night? What if he'd agreed only to spy on the dumpy ex-wife, not bed her?

Troy had believed Jackson's appearance at the Silver Spoon with an offer to help and an olive branch in hand was simply too fishy. And now she felt like a fool for not heeding her brother's sage warning.

"Savannah, please. You have to believe me."

He reached to draw her into his embrace, but Savannah swatted his hands away. "Don't touch me!"

"This is why I hesitated to tell you. I figured you'd react this way and I wanted you to get to know me better. Don't you see?"

"I have to get out of here." Savannah fumbled for the handle, pushed the door open and stalked toward her restaurant, ignoring Jackson's pleas.

CHAPTER 9

Angelica hated Monday mornings. She especially loathed the Monday mornings that followed jacked-up weekends, she thought as she moved toward the *Tribune*'s brightly lit coffee alley. Because she'd been running late for a photo shoot that was scheduled to begin in ten minutes, she hadn't had time to swing by Starbucks to pick up her favorite morning pick-me-up. She removed a small Styrofoam cup from the tall stacks leaning atop the counter like mini Towers of Pisa. The newsroom brew would taste like warm kerosene, but she would risk the damage to her taste buds for the much-needed caffeine jolt. That disaster of a date with Vince kept crowding her mind. She should've known a guy like him would have only one thing on his mind—trying to break a world's record for separating his dates from their panties. Still, regret gnawed at her. Not just because she had been duped into believing Vince Lomax actually liked her as a person, but because during dinner at Cesaro's she'd thought she caught a glimpse beyond "Low Max, the newsroom Lothario."

During dinner, before he'd gotten a tad too frisky with that crab leg and raspberry pastry, she'd actually enjoyed his company. He'd shared stories about his European travels. They'd compared notes about their frequent excursions to the Big Apple, and who would've thought they would both list *L.A. Confidential, The Usual Suspects* and *Reservoir Dogs* among their current top ten movie picks. Angelica sipped her coffee as she replayed their laughter when they both ripped into *Titanic* for winning an Academy Award for Best Picture, when the more deserving *L.A. Confidential* got stiffed and had to settle for bes adapted screenplay as a consolation prize.

And something else bugged her. She had sexed up her look to ensnare Jackson. He hadn't responded, but she'd become enraged and offended when Vince had.

How fickle was that?

"Angelica, your model is here." Abigail peered into the coffee alley. "I sent her back to the photography studio."

"Be right there." Angelica slugged the rest of the too-bitter coffee just before tossing the empty cup into a nearby trash can.

Angelica stepped into the photography studio and found Vince alone, rifling a roll of backdrops. "What are you doing in here?" she barked. "And what did you do with my model?"

"The model left to go to the powder room. When I walked by I heard obnoxious gagging sounds. I'm pretty sure she was barfing up that single Cheerio she probably had for breakfast. If you ask me, she doesn't look too good."

"Where's Sam? He's supposed to shoot for me today."

"Called in sick. I'm taking over all his assignments today," Vince replied with a surly look. He obviously wasn't too thrilled about the situation either.

"What about Adam?" The caffeine hadn't had a chance to kick in yet and Angelica's temples threatened to throb with a migraine.

"He's covering the Chandler trial at the courthouse."

"And Siegenthaler?"

"Shooting a bad rush-hour pile-up on I-75 North." Vince climbed a small stepladder and adjusted a strobe.

Angelica opened her mouth, but Vince cut her off. "Look, before you run down the entire *Tribune* photography staff, save your breath. I've already tried to get you another substitute. No one else is available. You're stuck with me or you're free to reschedule."

Angelica considered that option, then recalled that the Face Forward Modeling Agency contract she'd signed stipulated that the billing started as soon as the model arrived. Angelica had booked the session in advance, which meant the newspaper was obligated to pay the agency the full fee regardless of whether the photo shoot took place that morning or not. Damn! Nothing left to do but forge ahead like the professional she was. "Fine, you do the shoot,"

Angelica relented. "The sooner we get this over with, the better."

The mannequin-for-hire returned, dressed in a Juicy Couture tiny tee, which revealed her concave belly. Her trendy low-riding jeans clung to jutting hipbones that could be classified as lethal weapons. She fingered through a small tin Altoids box, then tossed several mints inside her mouth before offering Angelica her hand. Though she stood five feet ten in her sneakered feet, the flat-chested, freckle-faced girl looked as if she couldn't have been a day over fifteen, and she was way too skinny.

When Angelica had scanned the stack of Face Forward models' composite cards, the thick layers of foundation, smoky liner, spidery glued-on lashes and silicone falsies the girl had obviously stuffed in her training bra had added about a decade to her look.

As a former fashion model, Angelica knew modeling was a business that thrived on illusion, thinness and, most of all, youth. She'd also started young.

By the time Angelica had turned eighteen she'd left Cincinnati and relocated to New York, where most of her earnings had been snorted up her nose. The "happy dust" not only dulled the pain of the constant rejection that was inherent to the modeling industry, but it helped keep her weight in its most marketable range. For her medium-boned, five-foot ten-inch frame, that ridiculous range required that she weigh no more than one hundred and ten pounds. "The camera adds ten pounds" had been her modeling agent's mantra.

To land those more lucrative lingerie modeling gigs, Angelica had paid to have saline pouches stuffed where perfectly fine 34Bs had once been. These days, Angelica shuddered in disbelief when she unearthed old photos of herself looking so frighteningly malnourished—despite fake boobs so big they always appeared on the verge of exploding.

The craziness had finally come to an end when the real world called. She hit has-been classification at the age of twenty-four. Fortunately, her father had had the foresight to place a big chunk of her teen earnings in a great mutual find. By the time the modeling gigs completely dried up, she had a nice nest egg with which to finance her own college education.

The girl offered a hand so skeletal, Angelica feared a good firm grip might snap a bone. "Hi, I'm Kharisma, with a K."

Angelica nixed asking the girl if her mother had named her after a cheap drugstore cologne.

"Hello, Kharisma with a K, I'm Angelica Alexander, *Tribune* fashion editor." Angelica tamped down her courteous smile, then grudgingly continued the intros, gesturing in Vince's direction without sparing him a glance. "Kharisma, this is the photographer, Vince Lomax."

"Nice to meet you, Mr. Lomax."

"Vince is fine," he said to Kharisma before turning to Angelica, who could feel the full blast of his arctic glare. "I have to go and fetch another light meter. I'll be right back."

"How old are you?" Angelica asked after Vince left the studio.

"Fourteen and a half."

"How did you get here?"

"I rode the city bus." Kharisma crunched on the mouthful of Altoids.

"What about school?"

"I'm going." Kharisma sighed with a burst of potent peppermint. "I'm just going to be late. I have an excuse. It's fine. The semester ends in a week. Besides, I don't even know why I have to bother with school anyway. I'm going to be the next Iman or Tyra Banks. An agency in New York is interested in representing me and I'm moving there for the summer to build up my book and do go-sees. Isn't that way cool?"

Angelica didn't want to burst the girl's bubble by revealing to her that the "way cool" summer would possibly involve sharing a two-bedroom, five-story walk-up, a hot plate and one bathroom with ten Christy Turlington wannabes and an army of cockroaches. "Is that right?" Angelica replied with an indulgent smile instead.

They seemed to be recruiting them for high fashion at even younger ages, Angelica thought with dismay. Angelica still bore the battle scars of her own stint before the camera and on the catwalk. But now that she was no longer in a position to be exploited herself, she was guilty of perpetrating the same unhealthy images that forced her to do drugs to stay super thin and go under the knife to plump up her God-given assets.

She selected and rubber-stamped every model who appeared on the *Tribune* fashion pages. And what had she done to make a difference? She hadn't hired many models with realistic body types. She'd always chosen girls who looked frighteningly thin like Kharisma.

The realization disturbed her, but there was nothing she could do about that now. She had a photo shoot to complete if she was going to make her deadline for the section. Angelica reached for the bag on a table and removed a skimpy metallic bathing suit. "I need you to change into this. It's going to be the cover shot for our upcoming summer swimwear tabloid section."

"Wow!" Kharisma's hazel eyes widened. "I didn't know I was going to be a cover girl! That's going to be great for my modeling portfolio!"

Angelica watched the girl slip inside the studio's powder room to change, then took a seat.

Vince returned wielding another light meter. "Where's Kharisma?"

"You mean baby Twiggy?" Angelica replied with a frown.

Vince shushed her. "She might hear you."

"Yeah, you're right. It's not funny. It's sad actually."

"You're concerned about her, aren't you?" Vince asked as he positioned a Nikon atop a tripod, then adjusted the blue-sky backdrop a couple of feet away. The whizzing sound of rewinding film inside his camera filled the studio.

"Yeah, she reminds me of myself at that age." Angelica's unease regarding the girl suddenly overrode her grudge against Vince.

"If the poor kid wasn't so undernourished-looking that might not be such a bad thing," Vince replied with a small grin.

"Sounds as if you might be ready to bury the hatchet and move beyond that little run-in with my lawn sprinklers." She flipped her thick mane over one shoulder.

"Are you?" he tossed back with a sexy gleam in his eyes. "Willing to bury the hatchet somewhere besides my head, I mean?"

Before she could reply, Kharisma returned with swatches of the golden fabric crisscrossing her twig-like torso. The shimmering bathing suit wasn't designed for the water. Even its label warned "dry clean only."

Noshing on a doughnut, Abigail appeared in the doorway of the studio. "Wanted you guys to know our resident food critic just arrived with six dozen boxes of free Krispy Kremes."

"Krispy Kremes?" Kharisma swallowed audibly, then went slack-jawed with longing as she eyed the sugar-glazed piece of heaven in Abigail's hand.

"Yes, would you like one, young lady?" Abigail asked.

Kharisma bit her lip and shuffled her feet as if waging a battle with herself. "Um…no…no thank you."

"Jackson deposited them in the coffee alley. Better get 'em while they're hot…and before they're gone." Abigail pushed the last two bites of the treat inside her mouth.

Angelica rubbed her hands together in unveiled glee. "My favorite. You know I can't resist—"

"Another chance to drool over the doughnuts…or Jackson DeWitt?" Vince cracked, officially ending their tenuous truce.

With a wicked smile, Angelica launched a counter attack. "Abigail, did you know ol' Vince here had a penchant for mauve underpants?"

"Oh, my!" Abigail clutched the pearls around her neck in surprise.

"'Oh, my' is just what Angie said the other night," Vince fired back. "Just before I nibbled off the mauve edible pair she wore just for me. Get-your-groove-on grape, I believe they were, right, Angie?" He winked at Angelica.

Angelica, aghast that she'd left herself wide open for that zinger, was poised to deploy another one when Abigail cleared her throat and reminded them that a minor was in their midst.

Practically twitching with the need to have the last word, Angelica could feel Vince's cocky smirk. But she realized Abigail was right. They had to behave like adults—especially in front of the child.

Angelica glanced at Kharisma, sneered at Vince, then excused herself to grab a doughnut instead.

CHAPTER 10

That afternoon at the Silver Spoon Savannah marveled at how the lunch crowd nearly swelled the restaurant to capacity.

If she could maintain such a steady stream of customers through the rest of spring into the summer months, her restaurant would be well on its way to inching out of the red.

Troy took a break and left the hosting station to join Savannah in her office after the initial lunch rush. "This is great, isn't it?"

Savannah sat before her computer, surveying her work from the previous night. She'd been so distracted by that last disturbing conversation with Jackson, she felt compelled to check her entries. Erroneous data would wreak havoc on her books somewhere down the line.

Troy sat in a chair across from her and supped on the day's Silver Spoon lunch special—vegetable lasagna and thick slices of Italian bread. "I hate to admit this, but your new boyfriend's advice has been good for this place."

"He's not my boyfriend," Savannah said tightly as she jabbed at her keyboard.

"Your new associate, whatever you want to call him." Troy dug into his food with a fork. "I was a little hard on him at first, but most of his ideas, especially recruiting Eloise to revamp the entire menu and work with Percy and Emma Jean, were brilliant."

Great, Savannah thought with a rueful sigh. The irony of it all was too much. Just when she needed to purge her misgivings about Jackson, the one person who hadn't been immediately bamboozled by the man's guile was suddenly a convert.

Troy shoveled a big hunk of lasagna into his mouth. "Hmmp. Hmmp. Hmmp." His eyes rolled in obvious bliss. "Damn, Eloise is good. Forget the age gap, if the woman wasn't married I'd be on bended knee. Hey, I forgot to ask. Did Jackson mention that idea he had about hiring a jazz trio to play here on Saturday nights? I think that'll pull in folks who aren't just interested in good food. Man, that Jackson is really on top of it."

Convert? Scratch that. Her brother was now the newest card-carrying member of the Jackson DeWitt fan club. When had that happened? she wondered. Why, three weeks ago, Troy was shooting Jackson withering stares.

"I got to thinking. I was being a little too territorial with the dude at first," Troy began as if he'd read Savannah's mind. "And there was some of that brotherly over-protectiveness in the mix as well. But I'd say Jackson has more than proven he's a straight-up sorta guy who wants the best for you and this place. I mean, all of his advice, so far, has been right on the money, wouldn't you say? Business is steadily increasing with each passing day. And you can't argue with the results." Troy bit off a chunk of his bread.

Her brother's comments only confused Savannah more.

If Bryce or the *Tribune* bigwig had ordered Jackson to cozy up to Savannah to make sure she and the Silver Spoon failed, why hadn't he attempted to steer her in the wrong direction with bad advice? She tried ignoring that part of her that so desperately wanted to believe Jackson's version of the story.

Her restaurant was thriving, but the bottom line was he'd been dishonest, withholding vital information from her. Savannah clung to righteous indignation, disregarding the fact that she hadn't been completely forthcoming either. She'd gone out of her way not to mention her ex's name. And it had become a trap that had ensnared Jackson. In his lies? Or simply well-meaning omissions?

She contemplated going to Bryce, to put him on the spot. And simply ask him about Jackson point-blank, then try to glean something, anything, from Bryce's knee-jerk reaction.

Savannah dismissed that lamebrain idea. Her ex had been damn near pathological where she was concerned as of late. What would prevent him from lying? And why would Bryce Martin, of all people, crack under her interrogation? If anything, he'd get a big kick out of making her squirm. Hell, no. She would not give him the satisfaction.

Troy filled his fork with more pasta, but this time he leaned forward and guided it toward Savannah's mouth. "Here, you look like you could use a bite."

"No, thank you." She hadn't had much of appetite that day.

"You don't know what you're missing."

"I'll have some later," Savannah promised, distracted. "Troy, do you mind taking that in the kitchen? I need a few minutes."

"Sure thing," he said around a mouthful of lasagna as he stood. "Break's almost over anyway." At the door he turned to face her again. "You sure you're okay? You don't look so good."

"I'm fine," she said, giving him a wan smile. "Just a little tired. I didn't sleep very well last night."

Once Savannah was alone she simply stared at the phone on her desk. She reached for the receiver, then plopped it back in the cradle.

"Call him," the little voice in her head beseeched. "Have a civil conversation with the man and don't stop until all your nagging questions have been answered to your satisfaction." How many times had misunderstandings and assumptions wrecked promising new relationships?

But was it the voice of reason she heard? Or the siren's song of raging hormones trying to lure a lonely, sex-deprived divorcee back into Jackson's strong arms?

Savannah placed a hand on the phone again, letting her fingers curl around the receiver. Its sudden vibrating jangle startled her. She jumped, knocking it off its cradle. It clattered across the desktop as she fumbled to lift it to her ear. As always, she removed the gold bauble clipped to one lobe and answered with a cheerful, "The Silver Spoon Café."

"Savannah?" Jackson's clipped baritone came through. "We need to talk."

Still unsure how to proceed, Savannah didn't reply.

"Are you still there?" Jackson prodded. "I'm on my way over there now and I'm not leaving until we talk."

There was a click, then the dial tone hummed in her ear. She replaced the receiver, contemplating her options. She could make it harder on him and leave before he arrived. But how silly was that? This was her restaurant and Jackson wasn't running her off.

The sensible thing to do was to simply put her insecurities in check and hear Jackson out.

When Jackson appeared at the Silver Spoon's entrance, he suggested that Savannah follow him to his car.

Savannah hesitated momentarily, unsure whether being alone with him would cloud her reasoning.

Jackson sensed her obvious reluctance. "I'm not going to kidnap you. I just thought you might like the privacy, in case you want to yell at me some more."

Savannah followed him to his gleaming Acura. The vehicle always looked as if he'd just rolled out of a full-service car wash, where it had been waxed and buffed with meticulous care.

Once inside, Savannah aimed her gaze forward. She just wanted to hear his explanation, not become bewitched by those lethally sexy brown eyes of his.

"I hope you've had a chance to think about what I said last night," Jackson started. "I admit I was wrong for not telling you up-front what I'd heard your ex-husband was up to. But all I had to back me up was a hunch and some newsroom gossip. I didn't have any real proof. It's not as if my publisher mentioned Bryce Martin's name to me. And he never tried to dictate what I actually wrote in that review…I'm guessing it's because he knew I was panning the Silver Spoon anyway."

"Which is exactly what he and my ex wanted," Savannah reminded him.

"You've got to believe I wasn't in cahoots with the two of them. If I were trying to take you down, would I give you sound advice? Think about it? Does that make any sense?"

"It would if you were trying to lull me into a false sense of security before you sank the knife in my back."

"What could I possibly have to gain by being your ex's spy?" Jackson's tone thickened with frustration.

"You'd keep your publisher happy, which means you'd get to keep your job skewering restaurants for a living."

"Savannah. Let's get real here." Jackson reached over and angled her chin, forcing her to look him in the eyes. "I know we haven't known each other all that long, but I felt something special happening between us. And I know you felt it, too. Take a chance. Go with what I know your heart must be trying to tell you."

Jackson closed the distance between them, leading with his lips. Savannah's parted in anticipation. How badly she wanted him to kiss all her suspicions away.

He pressed his soft lips to her cheek, then his breath sent tingles through her body when he whispered against her skin, "I know you're frightened and you don't know what to believe or who to trust with a man like Bryce Martin conspiring against you. I don't blame you. But please, all I'm asking for is the benefit of the doubt. Can you do that much for me?"

Stunned by the raw sincerity she heard in his plea, Savannah nodded.

Jackson gently grazed his clean-shaven cheek against hers, then went for her mouth. His tongue swept inside, slowly, skillfully deepening the kiss by dizzying degrees. Savannah melted against him, curling her arms around his muscular shoulders. Soon, she was breathless and aching for more than he could offer in the front seat of a car in broad daylight.

Minutes later, Jackson broke the kiss long enough to issue an invitation. "I want you to go away with me this weekend. Any talk about the newspaper or the restaurant is forbidden. No business and no interruptions. Just you and me at this beautiful bed and breakfast about seventy miles outside of town. We need this time alone. Please say yes…" He traced a finger along her bottom lip. "For us."

"Is there really an us?"

"Yes, we're a couple, even if you don't want to believe it yet. It's just a matter of time until you do, and I'm not giving up."

"You really want to be with me?" Savannah asked, loathing how vulnerable and uncertain she sounded.

"Yes. Why is it so hard for you to believe that there are no ulterior motives here—beyond learning everything there is to know about you and getting so close we won't know where I stop and you begin." He smiled, then drew her deeper into his embrace.

"I—I don't know," she demurred.

"C'mon. Take a chance. I just want to spend some downtime with you in a beautiful, tranquil setting. No pressure. You can even have your own room."

"Hmmm, a bed and breakfast place. That does sound like fun."

"So, is that a yes?" He kissed the top of her head and tousled her cropped curls with his fingers.

Savannah gazed up at the man who was working his way into her heart and soul so rapidly it made her anxious, but obviously not enough to decline the romantic rendezvous.

"Me and you at the bed and breakfast this weekend. Is it a date?"

Savannah moved closer, enjoying the clean, masculine scent of his cologne. "It's a date."

During the drive home Jackson tried to concentrate on the happiness and relief he felt now that he and Savannah had made up. But soon another worry rattled him. He'd plan a romantic weekend getaway because he thought it was exactly what they needed to build a strong foundation for their fledging relationship. He wouldn't make any assumptions about how far they would take the physical intimacy. That would be Savannah's call. And he'd give her the option of having her own room so there wouldn't be any pressure on her. Still, he questioned whether he was really ready for what a rendezvous at the Grand Gables bed and breakfast could mean if she chose to share a room with him. A part of him hoped she would. He desired Savannah like no woman he'd ever encountered before. But on the other hand, was that alone enough to push him over that wall of doubt and insecurity? He'd dreamed of her every night and most mornings he'd awakened in need of a cold shower. He wouldn't obsess about this, he decided. He'd only focus on what was right between them.

They were going to have a wonderful weekend at Grand Gables.

CHAPTER 11

By the time Friday rolled around Savannah was more than ready for her getaway. While waiting for Jackson to arrive, she sat in her office at the Silver Spoon, adding last-minute reminders to a list for Troy.

"Here's the number where I can be reached. If there's an emergency, don't hesitate to call." She passed the sheet of paper to Troy.

He quickly perused it. "Whoa. So Jackson's taking you to the Grand Gables Bed & Breakfast in Perryvale. Not too shabby. Sounds as if things might be getting serious. I mean, from what I understand, it's a very romantic setup. I've heard folks say if you're not in love when you arrive, you will be by the time you leave. So what's the story there, sis? I know you were hankering for someone to date, but are we talking more than fun and recreation here? Are you starting to fall for this dude or what?"

Savannah had to take a minute. "I think I might be. God help me, because I still don't know if that's a smart move right now. It all seems to be happening so fast, ya know. It's a little scary."

"There are no time tables when it comes to love. Sometimes it just grabs you—almost by the throat— when you least expect it and won't let go."

"Tell me about it. But I've decided I'm not going to fight what's developing between Jackson and me."

"He makes you happy, doesn't he?"

Savannah didn't have to think too long there. "Yes, so far he has made me very happy. But a part of me almost feels as if he's a little too perfect. And I can't help thinking there's something inherently wrong with that."

"Sounds to me like a case of you not believing you deserve to be happy. And you do, sis. More than anyone I know, so go on and get yours!" He moved to wrap Savannah in a hug. "If that's Jackson, and he continues to treat you right, I'm all for it."

"I'm just going with the flow and hope I don't drown." The two moved apart when a knock sounded at the door.

"Come in," Savannah called out, sitting down behind her desk.

Clara poked her head inside. "Savannah, may I see you for a minute?"

"Well, back to the grind." Troy was about to skirt Clara when he stopped and placed a hand on her shoulder. "Hey, you all right?"

Clara's eyes were puffy and red, as if she'd been crying. "I'll take care of this, Troy," Savannah said. "Come inside, Clara, have a seat."

The woman did as instructed, blowing her nose into a tightly wadded Kleenex.

Savannah reached into her bottom drawer, removed a box of tissue, then placed it on her desk. "What's wrong, Clara?"

"It's Mikey. He's not doing so good. His condition took a turn for the worse last night and…" When Clara began to sob in earnest, Savannah left her chair and wrapped an arm around the woman's quavering body.

"It's all right. It's all right. Just let it all out." Savannah held her tightly, hoping the woman would draw some comfort from the embrace.

After a few minutes Clara gathered enough composure to speak. "See, Mikey has cerebral palsy."

"I didn't know." Savannah continued to rub Clara's back in a consoling manner.

"He was doing better there for a while, but now…" She sniffled. "He's hit a real tough stretch."

"Who cares for him when you and your husband are at work?" Savannah asked, assuming the couple could not afford in-home professional assistance.

Clara blew her nose with a honking snort. "When he's not in the hospital, my mother-in-law takes care of him. But she's not feeling too well today. She has a real bad bug or something and we're all awfully afraid she might give it to Mikey. He's in such a weakened state and all, something like this could be really bad for him."

"Clara, I'm so sorry. Is there anything I can do?" Savannah reached for a fresh tissue and passed it to the woman.

Clara's body jerked with more sobs. "Well, I was wondering if…I really don't want to be a bother."

"Go on, Clara."

"I need a few days off to take care of Mikey, at least until my mother-in-law is feeling better."

"Is that all? Of course, you can have a few days off for something like this. Everybody here likes you and I doubt there'll be a problem drafting someone to take your shifts, especially under the circumstances."

"Oh, Savannah, thank you." The woman's face brightened with a watery smile. "I was afraid that you'd be sorry that you hired me, that if I asked for any more special favors you'd fire me."

"Fire you? No way. You've done such a great job. I've tried very hard to create a family-like atmosphere here. And I always want my employees to feel as if they can come to me when they have problems. And that's what you did. Thanks for trusting me with the truth. You know, a lot of folks would've simply waited until the last minute to phone in sick."

"So you don't think I'm more trouble than I'm worth?"

"No way!" Savannah gave her a big smile. "You take care of your son, and don't worry about your job. It'll be here when you're ready to come back. Will you be finishing your shift or do you need to leave right away?" Savannah went to check the wait staff scheduling board mounted on the wall. "Let's see, JoAnne is scheduled to come in an hour, so it's not a problem if you have to leave immediately."

"I'll wait for JoAnne."

"Great."

"I don't know how to thank you. I'd better get back to the dining room." Clara went to the door.

"And oh, Clara. I'll make sure those Silver Spoon specials are delivered to your place while you're away."

Clara thanked her with another teary-eyed smile.

Savannah sat at her desk again. She'd just said a quick prayer of thanks for the many blessings she'd received and the opportunity to spread her own when the tranquility of her small office was shattered.

A nightmare suddenly materialized in the flesh. Savannah gasped and jumped. The door barely bracketed Bryce's tall, lanky form. He had to duck to clear the frame.

"Get off my property!" Savannah shrieked before he had a chance to open his mouth.

"Is that any way to greet the man who was once the love of your life?"

"You mean the louse of my life," Savannah corrected him. As she looked into the depth of those dark, reptilian eyes of his, she couldn't believe she'd ever deluded herself into believing she loved him.

"You've got yourself a real nice place here." He surveyed his surroundings before helping himself to a seat. "Don't forget you got the place because of me."

"And it's still open in spite of you. I know what you've been up to." Savannah couldn't get it out fast enough. "I knew you were spiteful enough to sit around hoping I'd fall on my ass with this venture, but I had no idea even you would go so low as to pull out all the stops, calling in old favors to try and make it happen."

Bryce went with mock surprise, but Savannah wasn't buying it.

"I have no idea what you're talking about. And I'm appalled that you think I would begrudge your happiness."

"Please. Don't even try it. I know all about your connection to an executive buddy at the *Tribune* and the role you played in making sure they reviewed the Silver Spoon." Savannah added a humorless chuckle. "So don't try denying it."

"I won't," he said breezily. "I did ask a friend to make sure your restaurant was reviewed. I thought it might be good publicity for the place. I swear, I had no idea that reviewer would be so vicious."

"Yeah, right," Savannah scoffed. "You must think I have risotto for brains. You must've forgotten all about that conversation where you didn't wish anything but doom-and-gloom on me and this restaurant. Now, all of a sudden I'm supposed to believe you're actually pulling for its success?'

He stood. "Oh, babe, I don't blame you for being suspicious. I mean, the last time we spoke I was still fuming because you walked out on me. I'd lost the one woman in my life who I'd ever loved. I was angry and hurt. I wanted to hurt you, too. I was only lashing out."

Savannah's jaw dropped. "Un-be-lie-va-ble."

"What? That I still love you, that I still care, that I want another chance with you?"

"I think you'd better leave."

"Please hear me out." Bryce closed the space between them and tried to reach for her hands.

Savannah grabbed a letter opener from the pencil holder on her desk and aimed the pointed end at his crotch. "Don't," she bit out with a warning glare, "touch me."

"So, after all we once meant to each other, we can't even have a civil conversation without you trying to shish kebab the family jewels?"

"Just keep your mitts to yourself." She held onto the letter opener as if she meant business.

"So what you're trying to say is we can't even be friends?"

"Absolutely not. Not friends, not acquaintances, not anything," Savannah replied without a hint of regret or uncertainty. She couldn't even remember why she even let the creep into her life the first time around. What had she been thinking? There was no way in hell she'd make the same mistake twice.

"What if I told you I made a mistake and that I still love you. I take the blame for everything that went wrong between us," he pleaded.

"I'd ask what you'd been smoking."

"But…but…"

"No buts, Bryce. It's crystal clear to me what this is about. Because I know you, the real you now. This is about me walking out on you. It still chaps your butt to no end that I was the one who left first. I filed for divorce. Your bloated ego just can't handle it. It's not enough that you lied to our mutual friends and told them you filed for the divorce. I didn't even try to correct that version of the story that got whispered around in your hoity-toity circles. Having revisionist gossip on your side was not enough, oh no. You couldn't stand that the one person you didn't want to know the real deal, knew the real me! So now you think you can just waltz back into my life, play nicey-nicey to lure me back into your little web, but only long enough so you can finally have the opportunity to kick me to the curb."

"It's not like that at all," Bryce insisted. "But I realize I can't just show up here and dump all this on you without expecting some resistance. You're going to need some time."

Someone interrupted with a tap on the door.

"Come in," Savannah called out.

Clara stepped inside. "Sorry to interrupt you, Savannah, but Jackson DeWitt is waiting for you out front. He said to bring some of Eloise's chocolate chip cookies to snack on during the drive."

"Thanks, Clara." Savannah's mood rallied and she quickly cleared her desk. "Tell him I'll be right out."

Bryce obviously noted the abrupt change in her demeanor. "Jackson DeWitt? Isn't that the guy who trashed your restaurant in the *Tribune*?"

"Yes," Savannah chirped.

"So you two are chummy now?"

Savannah paused and tilted her head thoughtfully. "More like very chummy." She didn't owe Bryce any updates on her social life, but she simply couldn't pass up an opportunity to rub it in. He also needed to know that reconciliation wasn't happening in this lifetime.

Savannah reached for the small suitcase under her desk. She'd packed it for her weekend trip, but hadn't left it in her car trunk. The late May sun would have melted her cosmetics.

"You're going away with him?" Bryce's nostrils flared. "I don't believe this."

Savannah locked her desk drawers and standing file cabinets, then went to the door with her suitcase. "We're not married anymore. What I do is no longer your concern. Don't you have some skinny, rich socialites to stalk?"

Savannah recognized the storm brewing in Bryce's eyes and instinctively knew his claims of being a changed man were a load of bunk. "You're making a big mistake," he fumed.

Savannah lifted a brow. "Is that another threat?"

"Of course not," Bryce managed as if measuring his words. "You just need time."

"I wouldn't hold my breath if I were you. I'm on my way out. I'll escort you."

❧

Savannah climbed inside Jackson's car prepared for a flurry of questions about the man who had accompanied her out of the Silver Spoon. Instead, he greeted her with an inviting smile and hug.

"Ready for our trip?"

"Yes, I've been counting the hours." Savannah secured her seatbelt.

"Me, too. I think it'll be a weekend neither of us will soon forget."

Jackson gave Savannah a look that that made her blush.

Unless Jackson was a phenomenal actor, which she didn't believe for a minute, his lack of a reaction to seeing Bryce was all the proof she needed. Giving Jackson the benefit of the doubt had been a good call. He really hadn't been in cahoots with her ex-husband. In fact, he didn't appear to even recognize him.

As Jackson guided the car along the ramp leading to the highway, curiosity got the best of her. She opened the topic for discussion. "Aren't you going to ask me about that guy I was chatting with as I left the restaurant?"

"Not to sound too cocky or anything, but you're going away with me for the weekend. And as far as I'm concerned, that's all that matters. But I'll bite.

Was he a smitten customer trying to get your home phone number? You deal with the public in your line of work. I'm sure male diners hit on you all the time. Any man involved with you just has to get used to it."

Savannah dropped "That was Bryce" like an anvil.

"Oh?" Jackson replied in an even voice, though Savannah noted how his grip on the steering wheel tightened. "What did he want? You didn't invite him there, did you?"

"No."

"What did he want?"

"He claims another chance." Savannah flipped down the sun visor flap and checked her hair in its mirror.

"With you?"

"Yes."

"And you told him to go to hell, right?"

"Thought you weren't worried about competition because you had me for the weekend?" Savannah smiled.

"An ex-husband is a whole 'nother story. Sometimes it's impossible to compete with history."

She placed her hand on his thigh. "Just teasing you. I'm so over Bryce and his bull."

CHAPTER 12

A little more than two hours later they arrived at the Grand Gables Bed & Breakfast, an early-1900s two-story manor tucked amid a grove of century-old oak trees.

"This is lovely!" Savannah bounded out of the car.

"I thought you'd like it." Jackson popped the trunk, grabbed their luggage, then followed her up the stone walkway leading to the planked porch. A stone-studded stream flowed to the right of the structure.

Inside, the owner of the inn, Barbara Lockhart, a Martha Stewart look-alike with a quick laugh, greeted them and removed a large leather-bound guest book to complete the registration. "Don't worry, we're fully computerized here," she explained. "And we accept all major credit and debit cards. I just like the nostalgia of having guests register the old-fashioned way."

After Jackson signed the necessary forms, Barbara lifted two leaf-shaped key rings from a drawer. Shiny keys to two rooms on different floors dangled from them.

Jackson and Savannah stood frozen, staring at each other awkwardly.

Barbara jangled the keys again.

Jackson took the keys from Barbara's hand. He sighed wearily and passed one to Savannah.

Jackson's obvious reluctance was the signal Savannah needed. She kept her gaze on him and dropped her key back into Barbara's hand—without a word.

Savannah's smile—along with Jackson's—said it all.

❦

Their room boasted a Jacuzzi, fireplace and an enormous feather bed. French doors opened to a balcony with a view of a meticulously maintained garden of vibrant lilies, hyacinths, daffodils and roses.

"Wow," Savannah whispered in wonderment. "Isn't the view wonderful?" She leaned against the banister and inhaled deeply, savoring the floral-scented air.

"Yes, exquisite." Jackson stood behind her, cradling her in his arms. "You get more beautiful to me with each passing day."

"I was talking about this view." She spread her arms wide with the spontaneity of a small child.

He turned her to face him. "It pales in comparison to you." Then he covered her lips with a long, deep kiss that left her practically panting for more. Down girl, she reminded herself, when she was nearly over-whelmed with the need to strip out of her clothes. They had all night. All weekend.

He led her back inside. "I arranged for you to have an aromatherapy soak in the Jacuzzi, then a full-body massage. I hope you don't mind my taking the initiative there." He glanced at his watch. "The masseuse should arrive in ten minutes."

"What will you do while I'm getting pampered?"

"Take a walk around, check out some things." He pecked her cheek. "There are more surprises where that masseuse came from."

"You're going to spoil me rotten."

"That's the plan," he said just before he answered the knock at the door.

A twenty-something woman was on the other side with a portable massage table and supplies.

Jackson looked over his shoulder at Savannah. "Enjoy. I'll return in a couple of hours, just in time for dinner."

❦

The secluded thickly wooded B&B property soon gave way to landscaped pastoral areas, as Jackson drove to town filled with anticipation. He passed a charming mix of brick, clapboard and Victorian homes populating the residential areas of Perryvale.

A few blocks from the town square, he left his car on a paved parking lot to stroll brick sidewalks that had more pedestrians than he'd expected.

Businesses were housed in a mix of traditional and contemporary buildings. He reached inside the pocket of his shirt and removed his shopping list for seduction. Seduction, he thought with a smile, as his excitement settled in his stomach causing a queasy sensation. His insides lurched. Nervous energy could do that to a person, he decided. That churning, anxious feeling was nothing more than that, he told himself. Savannah had opted to share a room and a bed with him. Yes! And he wanted to make this weekend absolutely perfect for her. He immediately spotted a florist where he purchased a fat bouquet of red roses. His portable CD player was in the trunk of his car, locked and loaded with Maxwell, Brian McKnight and D'Angelo. And who would even think of romancing a lady without classic Nat King Cole, Marvin Gaye and Barry White? Jackson quickly worked down his list, adding a bottle of Cristal and chocolate-covered strawberries to the bouquet. Once he found the candles, he could head back to Grand Gables.

"Excuse me." Jackson stopped a young woman holding a sleeping toddler on her hip. "Would you happen to know which one of these stores might carry candles?"

"What type of candles?" she asked. "Birthday cake candles? Roman candles like for fireworks?"

Jackson grinned. "Yeah, I guess you can say they're for fireworks. I'm trying to set the mood for a very special lady."

"Ohhhh." She nodded knowingly. "You want to go Trella's Treasure Trove. It's down at the end of this block on the right side." She pointed. "Looks as if you have just about have everything covered. Those flowers are gorgeous and they smell…" she sniffed a velvety bud, "they smell heavenly. Trella's will have anything else you need."

Jackson plucked one rose from the two dozen he carried and presented it to the young woman. "Thanks for your help." Then he turned and headed toward the recommended shop.

"Hey," the young woman called after him.

Jackson looked over his shoulder.

"Lucky girl!" She smiled, then disappeared in a cluster of pedestrians.

Trella's was one of those kitschy bric-a-brac places that Jackson usually avoided. Pop star posters adorned the walls. Gag gifts such as rubber vomit, whoopee cushions, hot pepper gum and whizzing cherubs lined the shelves. Rows of tacky greeting cards with explicit messages he'd never read in a Hallmark filled an entire wall.

A very tall woman, who a hunch told him was Trella herself, wore a platinum blond wig and an electric green jumpsuit. She called out to him from the rear of the store. "Be right with you in a sec." She had what he'd referred to as that hussy-husky quality to her voice a la Demi Moore and Kathleen Turner.

Jackson perused the wares, wondering why that woman with a baby had steered him here, of all places. The plan was to sweep Savannah off her feet with romance—not raunchiness.

There was a time when he could and would get buck wild with the best of them. But he had such high hopes for his relationship with Savannah, he was determined to approach their first time with more romance and reverence. They could save the games, gadgets and gizmos for later to keep things spicy.

Everything had to be perfect this weekend. His pulse quickened and his palms became sweaty the more he thought about it. He knew he was probably putting too much pressure on himself, but he couldn't help it. It had been seven long months since he'd been with a woman.

Green jumpsuit approached him, teetering on glittering platform shoes. The closer she got the more apparent it was that she was most definitely a he. Pudding thick brown makeup did a poor job of camouflaging the rugged terrain of a shaving-bumped jaw. An Adam's apple refused to be restrained by the beaded elastic choker encircling the neck. The man appeared to be in his early fifties, but it was quite possible the goopy makeup added a few years.

"What can I do for you?"

"I was told I could find some candles here," Jackson replied.

"You looking for scented, unscented, votives, stick? Candles in a tin or a jar?"

"May I look at what you have? I'll know it when I see it."

"Follow me."

Jackson did.

"Judging from that stash in your arms, I'm assuming you're setting a scene for seduction. Ohhh, my favorite pastime!" Jackson didn't reply immediately.

"Oh, c'mon, don't be shy. You can tell ol' Trella anything. As you can see, we have a wide variety of candles. The cinnamon-buns scented ones are my personal favorite."

Jackson plucked up four packages of six unscented votives—more than enough to place strategically around the room. "I believe these will work." The last thing he needed was to make Savannah nauseated if he chose the wrong scent.

Trella approved of his reasoning.

Jackson scanned the rest of the wares in the romance-a-rama section. He lifted a tin of something called Kama Sutra Honey Dust, which came with its own miniature feather duster.

"That's dee-lish." Trella bought one very large, manicured hand to his faux breasts. "Dust it on and lick it off. Tastes just like Honey Nut Cheerios."

"Is that right?" Jackson replaced the tin when a bottle of something labeled Rocket Booster captured his attention. "What's this?"

"A vitamin supplement. Puts more throttle in your thrust. More ka-blast in your ka-boom." Trella winked a garishly painted eye. "It's great."

"So you've used this?" Jackson was intrigued.

"My wife loves it when I do."

"You're married?" Jackson knew he shouldn't have assumed Trella wasn't. Men who had a penchant for women's clothing weren't necessarily gay.

Trella quickly scanned his store to be sure no one was eavesdropping on their private conversation before he continued with a conspiratorial whisper. "Yeah, see, Daisy is quite a few years younger than me and though I could usually hold my own with women my age, when I started dating Daisy I had to face a hard fact. I wasn't feeling quite as…um… What's the word?"

"Virile?" Jackson added.

"Yeah, that's it. Quite as virile as I used to."

Jackson thought it odd that a man who stuffed his Cross Your Heart Bra and reeked of Chanel No. 5 would fret about virility.

"Taking the tablets gave me that extra little edge I needed to keep my confidence—and another choice body part soaring. I rocked Daisy's world when I popped those pills and she ended up popping the question. He lifted a hand with shimmering lacquered nails to show off his "wedding band," which was actually Daisy's name tattooed around his hairy ring finger.

Jackson held on to the bottle, noting its $24.95 price tag.

Trella went into hard-sell mode. "Because you seem like such a nice young fella, I'll let you buy that bottle for a third off the marked price."

"Is this stuff safe?" Jackson found himself asking, despite his better judgment.

"I look as fit as a fiddle, don't I?" Trella lifted his hands dramatically.

Jackson quickly scanned the label, which only had one warning: Keep out of reach of children. "Sounds like Viagra."

"It's Viagra-like. You need a prescription for the real thing. This here's just a dietary supplement, perfectly harmless. It doesn't even have to be approved by the FDA. And I wouldn't be selling it in my store—or taking it—if I didn't trust and believe in it."

"And what is it exactly that puts more 'ka-blast in your kaboom?'"

"An all-natural herbal extract called yohimbe. It increases the blood flow…um…where you'll need it most."

Jackson flashed back to that night he and Savannah were going at it on his couch and how his confidence had lagged at the most inopportune time. Maybe having this Rocket Booster on hand would be just the little insurance he needed.

Jackson left Trella's Treasure Trove with his candles, flowers, champagne, chocolate strawberries and his secret weapon, which came in easy, digestible tablet-form. Stamina Man was back. One way or the other.

CHAPTER 13

At Grand Gables Jackson presented Savannah with the roses and the rest of the goodies he'd purchased.

They strolled around the beautiful grounds as the sun set, then settled on a secluded stretch of the property near a babbling spring.

They feasted on the delicious gourmet picnic Barbara had packed for them. After they'd stuffed themselves with roasted game hens and pasta salad, they ate plump chocolate-covered strawberries.

"This is heavenly," Savannah sighed as she reclined on the soft blanket spread across a patch of lush grass.

Jackson stretched out next to her. He'd propped himself up on elbow and now gazed into her eyes.

"I do love my pink sunsets."

"And I love you," he declared, his eyes dark with emotion.

The sincerity Savannah saw gleaming in his eyes made her heart turn over. "I love you, too." She reached up to curl her arms around his neck. He drew her closer and his lips locked onto hers.

His hands eased between them and slowly released the buttons of her blouse.

His mouth closed over the impression of one beaded nipple straining against the satin cup of her bra. His fingers sank into her hot flesh as she ran her tongue along his neck and gently nibbled at the sweet, salty taste of his silken brown skin.

He worked his way from her head to her toes, taking a leisurely pit stop at the juncture of her thighs, where the combination of his hot tongue and the slightly cool early evening breeze sent Savannah's world whirling into orbit. She raised her hips to meet him. The stubble of his slight five o'clock shadow added to his all-out tactile blitz in a surprisingly pleasant way. She would never think of razor stumble the same way again. She gasped, loving the feel of it gently abrading her delicate flesh. Only seconds later, a sweet fluttering sensation rippled from her core through her body. Heat pushed to her cheeks and a moan so protracted it sounded like a far-off echo fell from her lips. Blue sky seemed to melt into lush green earth from that highest pleasure peak.

She rode out the last waves of the most exquisite release; then whooped in surprise when he suddenly lifted her off the blanket and turned her over on her stomach. "What are you doing?" she chuckled.

"I'll give you a minute to catch your breath," he said in a thick whisper against her ear. "But I'm not done with you just yet."

An erection surged between Jackson's legs. He was ready. When he reached inside his pant pockets for a condom, his fingers brushed against the small bottle of insurance he'd stashed there—just in case. He felt good—just like his old self—in fact exactly like himself before he'd had that procedure seven months ago.

"Now, Jackson, now. I can't wait to feel you inside me," Savannah purred, spreading her thighs.

He could do this.

Couldn't he?

His heart rate increased and his breathing grew shallow. And he knew those reactions had nothing to the do with the lust thickening his blood. But he refused to choke again. He was determined to please his woman like never before. He fitted the condom over his erect penis, all the while telling himself he didn't need any crutches in the form of a supplement. But he still felt his confidence quickly skidding away.

"Now, Jackson now." Savannah raised the curves of her bottom toward him.

"Anticipation is part of the fun," he said as he reached back inside his pocket, removed the small bottle and tossed two Rocket Booster tablets inside his mouth and swallowed them dry. He felt the tablets make their slow descent down his throat. It would've been a hell of a lot easier if he'd washed them down with some warm champagne or something. But she couldn't suspect that he was taking something. He quickly folded an extra blanket into a tight compact pillow and tucked it beneath her belly and hips.

"Ready or not, here I come," he said, pressing himself against her, circling the moist entry of her body until she couldn't take the teasing anymore. He buried himself deep inside her, parting her softness and riding the warm cushioning contours of her voluptuous body until they both gasped in release.

On rubbery legs, Savannah followed Jackson back to their room. A lazy, satisfied smile parked on her face as she dropped onto their feather bed.

Making love to him had been more wonderful than she'd imagined. Not only had they shared a blistering passion, but the genuine emotion behind their bodies melting together in the most intimate way convinced her that she'd never feel this way about any other man. Jackson was the one. Finally. They were so perfect together in every way. As he approached her again with that hungry look in his eyes, she opened her heart completely and they took turns pleasuring each other's bodies again.

And again. And again.

A few hours later, after Savannah had fallen asleep, Jackson crept out of their warm bed and into a cold shower. A full erection still bobbed between his legs after three hours of lovemaking.

Jackson stepped out of the shower and dried off, still hard as a steel pipe. He quietly threw on a pair of shorts, T-shirt, and sneakers and slipped out of the room. A nice, long jog would relieve him, he thought, but when he returned an hour later after a seven-mile run his turgid penis was still penned against his stomach, restrained by the elastic waistband of his briefs.

He tiptoed back into their bedroom where he found Savannah still sleeping peacefully.

He removed his clothes, stepped into a cold shower again, then snuggled next to her underneath the sheets. But dozing off was impossible. He tried not to panic when he realized he had a problem. He'd maintained an erection for close to seven hours. He glanced at the clock, which read 3:02 a.m. He got up again, pacing the floor until he realized he had to get help.

※

Jackson sat in a clinic in Waverly, Ohio, the next town north of Perryvale. He'd awakened Barbara, who'd provided directions to the only 24-hour emergency room within a fifty-mile radius. The doctor's official diagnosis: priapism. Sounded like something Jackson had drawn with a pencil and protractor in his tenth grade geometry class. But the doctor went on to explain that it was actually a condition in which an erection lingered, sans sexual stimulation. It had likely been triggered not only by the yohimbe in those two Rocket Boosters he'd popped, but some weird interaction between the yohimbe and the prescription medication Jackson was still taking for the swelling in his prostate.

Stupid! Stupid! Stupid! Jackson flogged himself mercilessly as the doctor performed a quick, but unpleasant, procedure that involved long needles to relieve the unyielding pressure Jackson experienced below the belt.

After Jackson was done kicking himself, he wanted to plant his size-thirteens up a certain blonde shop-keeper's kiester.

Early the next morning, Savannah scooted across the bed, still struggling through a sleep haze. She tried snuggling into Jackson, but found his side of the bed empty.

She sat up, resting against the padded headboard and calling out to him. When she scrambled off the bed, she peeked into the bathroom. No Jackson. Maybe he went for an early morning jog, she decided, stepping inside the shower.

An hour later Savannah had dressed, but Jackson had yet to return.

When a knock sounded at the door, she went to open it with a big morning smile, sure Jackson had forgotten his key. Instead of Jackson, she found Barbara standing with a serving cart topped with silver trays of food.

"Good morning!" Barbara beamed, pushing the cart inside the room. "You know the five-course breakfast is complimentary. Would you two like to enjoy this in the room or out on the balcony?"

"The balcony would be nice," Savannah went to open the French doors.

Barbara positioned wicker chairs at each end of the cart, which would serve as their table, then proceeded to lift the domes off their dishes to reveal a veritable feast of crepes, eggs, bacon, sausage, fresh melon slices and blueberries. A crystal pitcher held fresh squeezed orange juice, chilled and thick with juicy pulp, just the way Savannah liked it.

"I can have a bottle of champagne delivered in case you two want to make mimosas." Barbara adjusted the centerpiece, a vase of fresh daisies.

"Darn, Jackson's not here," Savannah lamented. "The juice is going to get warm and the food cold."

"He's not back yet?" Barbara asked, her brow pleating with concern. "I noticed his car wasn't out front. I hope he wasn't seriously ill."

"Ill?"

"Yes, he knocked on my door early this morning inquiring about the nearest emergency room. I asked if he needed someone to drive him there, but he was adamant. He assured me that he could get there fine on his own. Now I wish I'd been more insistent, because he didn't look so good."

"Did he say what the problem was?"

"No. Just that he needed a doctor. I thought maybe he had a bug or something. You know how those things can hit out of the blue. If you want I can call the clinic to find out if he made it there all right."

"Would you?"

"Sure thing. I have the number in my office. I'll be right back."

Barbara departed, leaving the door wide opened.

Savannah didn't bother closing it as she concentrated on quelling her rising panic. What had happened to Jackson last night? And why didn't he wake her? She paced the room as a dozen questions whirled around in her head. She searched for a note. Maybe he'd left her one explaining everything. She pulled out the chair where Jackson had thrown the slacks he'd worn the day before. She draped the pants across the chair's back, then sat and searched through the slips of paper on top of the desk. When she reached for the notepad, the slacks slid to the floor. A small bottle fell out and rolled across the area rug with a rattle.

Savannah retrieved the slacks and the bottle, then took her seat again. Before she stuffed it back inside his pocket, the words on the label jumped out at her. "Rocket Booster?" she muttered as curiosity got the best of her. She quickly scanned its small print and discovered it was some sort of over-the-counter herbal supplement, which promised to enhance sexual performance.

"What the hell…?" Jackson stood in the doorway, glaring at her.

Jolted by his sudden reappearance, she pushed to her feet, releasing a jagged gasp.

He stalked across the floor and snatched the bottle out of her hands with such force she almost lost her balance. "What the hell do you think you're doing snooping through my things?"

His thick brows collided, his jaw clenched tight. She'd never seen him so angry.

"Jackson…I—I…was worried about you," she stammered. "I woke up and you weren't here…then Barbara came in and said you came to her last night asking about an emergency room. I didn't know what to think."

"So you thought you would find answers in my pants pockets? What exactly were you searching for, huh?" He quickly stuffed the bottle of tablets into the pocket of his shorts.

"It's not what you think…really…I…" Savannah tried to explain how his pants had fallen to the floor and the bottle of tablets rolled out.

Barbara reappeared. "Jackson! There you are." The bed and breakfast owner stepped inside the room. "I just called the clinic, but they refused to give me any information on you over the phone. Are you all right? I told Savannah here that you didn't look so good when you left here last night and—"

"And it would do wonders for this place if you could learn to keep your mouth shut and your nose out of your guests' business," Jackson bit out, startling Savannah and Barbara.

His words brought the inn owner up short. The pale woman's cheeks colored. "I—I'm sorry I didn't mean to—"

"Can you please give us some privacy?" Jackson cut her off with acid in his voice. Barbara quickly backed out of the room.

Savannah forgot that she had her own dispute to settle with Jackson, but rushed to the B&B owner's defense. "She was only trying to help. You disappeared without so much as a word. I was worried about you—especially after she told me you fell ill and needed a doctor. What was wrong? Is everything all right?"

Instead of answering her questions, he tried putting her on the defensive. "This is about you still not trusting me, isn't it?" Before she could reply, he continued his rant. "You know what? Never mind. I don't care anymore. I'm tired of pleading and begging, practically kissing your butt to convince you to believe in me."

Savannah couldn't believe her ears. "What?"

"You heard me. Enough is enough."

"What's come over you?" It was as if some alien asshole had taken possession of his body. "What are trying to say?"

"I'm not trying to say anything, I'm telling you I can't do this anymore."

It was as if he'd drop-kicked her in the chest. Savannah struggled to inhale her next breath.

He moved through the French doors and braced his arms against the banister on the balcony. "I don't think this is going to work." He refused to look at Savannah, instead gazing into the distance.

Anger, but mostly hurt, had Savannah reeling. She'd opened her heart and soul to this man. And this was how he responded? Like the typical commitment-phobic creep. He was obviously picking a silly fight to put some distance between them.

Before marrying Bryce she'd been in the dating game long enough to recognize the typical pursuit and panic dance. Now that they'd had sex and swapped the dreaded L-word, he'd grasp any flimsy excuse to jam on the brakes. As much as she loved him, she knew the worst thing she could do at this point was to get clutchy.

"Fine," she managed in a calm casual voice, despite the pain of her breaking heart. "Guess this means our weekend is over."

"I think that's best under the circumstances," he replied, keeping his back to her.

Savannah stared at his still, tall form, hoping she would awaken from this nightmare any minute.

"I'll give you some time alone to gather your things." He walked past her and out the door.

Still stunned, Savannah wasn't sure how long she stayed anchored at the same spot after the door closed behind him.

❧

Jackson ran the trail threading through the thicket of woods. The full weight of the humiliation he'd felt walking in to find Savannah standing there with that bottle of Rocket Booster in her hands bore down on him to the point that it felt if he didn't move, get as far as away from Savannah and Grand Gables as he could, he'd suffocate.

After about a half mile, he stopped to lean against a tree and catch his breath.

He'd felt helpless, out of control and numb in the crotch. He'd had to lash out.

He imagined Savannah telling her friends about the tablets she'd found in his pockets and having a good laugh at his expense. Or worse, he imagined the discovery turning her completely off to the point that she no longer saw him as a virile, desirable man. As much as it tore his heart out to end things the way he had, he needed to cling to a shred of his pride. He'd merely ended things with her before she could dump him.

When Jackson returned to Grand Gables an hour later, he found a cleaning lady in their room. The older woman appeared startled. "Sorry. Your lady friend checked out already. I assumed you had departed, too, so I came up to clean the room, then I noticed your things were still here. I was just leaving."

"Is the young lady waiting for me downstairs?" Jackson asked as he began gathering his belongings to stuff inside an overnight bag.

"I don't think so. I didn't see her in any of the lounging areas."

Jackson had had to get out of this room that had suddenly made him feel claustrophobic. Maybe Savannah had felt the same way, he decided.

Jackson finished packing, showered and dressed. Downstairs at the registration counter he looked out the windows, scanning the grounds for Savannah.

Barbara appeared. "She's gone."

"For a walk?" Jackson asked, suddenly feeling bad about the way he'd spoken to the B&B owner in the room earlier.

"No, she left for Cincinnati."

Jackson blinked. "Cincinnati?"

"How?"

"By taxi."

"That's going to cost a fortune."

"Guess she thought it was a small price to pay to be rid of you," Barbara said tartly as she completed his checkout.

"Look, Barbara, about what I said earlier."

Barbara lifted a hand to cut him off. "I'm not the one you should be apologizing to. You've paid your bill so we're square. But it's a shame that this expensive romantic weekend you planned—"

"Blew up in my face," Jackson completed the thought.

"True, but here's something to ponder during the lonely three-hour drive back to Cincinnati: Who pressed the detonator?"

CHAPTER 14

Angelica hadn't planned on using Kharisma for additional fashion layouts, but there the girl was preening in front of a backdrop aglitter with faux raindrops for an upcoming rainwear spread.

Since that swimsuit cover shoot, the kid had made a habit of phoning Angelica at the newsroom "just to chat."

On the Internet, the girl had stumbled across old photos of Angelica from her modeling days, and now she looked up to Angelica as a role model of sorts.

Though a part of Angelica was flattered by the girl's attention, it disturbed her that Kharisma was in awe of those old, coked-up images. The girl obviously had unhealthy habits and ideals regarding her own body. Angelica hoped she could use whatever influence she had over the girl to set her on the right path.

Vince stood behind a camera perched on a tripod clicking away and cracking jokes to keep Kharisma laughing.

Much to Angelica's surprise, he'd put their differences aside and volunteered for the job, claiming the rainwear shoot was preferable to another five-alarm fire or pileup on I-275. He just wasn't in the mood for gloom the first thing that Monday morning. Angelica suspected there was much more behind his newfound interest in fashion. He'd never admit to it, but he'd also taken an interest in Kharisma.

Angelica would've immediately made sure he didn't get within a mile of the girl if she'd suspected that his interest was improper. But she knew even Vince would not stoop so low as to hit on a minor. No way. There was something more behind the charm and attention he tossed the girl's way.

When Kharisma threw back her head to laugh at another one of Vince's corny jokes, she dropped the ornate parasol in her hand. She wobbled on thin legs as if she were dizzy.

"Are you all right, Kharisma?" Angelica asked.

"Y-yes. I'm fine." When the girl crouched to retrieve the prop, she collapsed to the floor.

Angelica lurched to her feet. "Kharisma!"

Vince raced over, calling the girl's name. He kneeled, gently placed her head on his lap, and reached for her wrist. "Her pulse is kinda weak. Better call an ambulance."

❦

Angelica and Vince sat in the waiting room of the hospital and watched Kharisma's mother pace, lost in her world of worry.

"I hope Kharisma's going to be all right," Angelica mumbled to Vince, who'd moved to the molded vinyl seat next to hers.

Vince leaned forward, resting his elbows on his thighs. "I think I know exactly what's wrong with Kharisma and I should've tried to do something sooner. I recognized all the signs, including the red marks on her knuckles."

"The scarring from jamming her fingers down her throat so many times to purge," Angelica added quietly.

"The sound of the long-running water when she'd duck into the powder room." Vince shook his head.

"To drown out the gagging sounds."

"She practically lived on breath mints."

"To mask the sour stench of the vomit on her breath."

"So we both suspected," Angelica said wearily.

Vince sat upright, fisting his hands. "I more than suspected and I should've acted more decisively and called her mother to tell her what I knew rather than dicking around waiting for God knows what to happen."

"If you were like me, maybe you were hoping you could forge a strong connection to get through to her. I got the impression that Kharisma has a strained relationship with her mother, which means she could possibly be the last person Kharisma is willing to listen to. And then there was the risk of alienating her further if she found out one of us snitched to her mom. At least you cared enough to think about trying. That counts for a lot." Angelica reached out and covered his hand with hers.

"No fair blaming yourself either." Vince threaded his fingers through hers, readily accepting the comfort she tried to offer. "Sounds like we both had good intentions, huh?"

Angelica gave him a small smile. "Uh-oh, I think the planets are aligning as we speak. Can you believe it? We're both on the same page for once."

Vince squeezed her hand. "Ya know, with that kinda cosmic good karma on our side, I'm not willing to think the outcome here will be anything less than positive. Kharisma is going to be fine."

"Damn right." Angelica felt hope rallying as a companionable silence stretched between them for the next hour.

Angelica eventually spoke again. "Vince, I know about eating disorders because of model friends who had them. Is that how you knew all that stuff about bulimia? By photographing models, I mean?"

"Not exactly." Vince paused, as if carefully measuring his words. "Someone I cared about once, she wasn't a model. In fact, she wasn't even sickly thin, but she suffered from the same eating disorder, only her case was worse."

"Worse?"

"Yeah, her body couldn't take the binge-and-purge abuse after a while." His voice thickened with emotion that he tried to conceal with an exaggerated clearing of his throat. "She died of heart failure."

"Vince, I'm so sorry." Angelica held onto his hand and squeezed.

"That was five years ago."

"Who was she?"

"My fiancée, Caitlin."

"You were engaged once?" Angelica didn't do a good job of hiding her surprise.

"Don't look so shocked." He seemed to take umbrage. "I am human. I have feelings and even old hard-hearted Vince fell in love once."

"It's just that…I mean… all those wild stories I've heard about your sexual escapades around the newsroom—"

"I'm not going to pretend some of it isn't true, but if I did everything I've been accused of, when would I find the time to eat, sleep and work? I've never bothered to try to deny the rumors because I figured what the hell, all the better to keep some emotional distance."

"So you won't be hurt again?" Angelica asked.

"Losing Caitlin almost did me in," he said quietly. "I'd thrown in the towel on relationships and love."

Seeing Vince in a whole new light, Angelica nodded in understanding. "I can still see the pain in your eyes when you speak of her. Caitlin must've been one special lady."

"Yes, she was. She didn't take any guff off me and didn't hesitate to bust my balls when I overstepped the boundaries. Sorta like a certain super-sexy fashion editor I know." He brought her hand to his mouth and planted a soft kiss there that brought a warm smile to Angelica's lips.

"You're such a man of mystery, Vince. Just when I think I've got you pegged…"

"Bam, huh?"

"Bam, exactly. You know, I've got something I should confess, too. I was giving you such a hard time for coming on so strong with the sexually charged flirting, when I'd done exactly the same thing with Jackson. Sorta makes me a bit of a hypocrite, don't you think?"

"Remember, you said it, I didn't. I don't want you coming after me with a fire hose next time."

"No more water attacks." Angelica lifted her free hand in oath.

"Since we're laying our cards on the table I have to reveal something as well," Vince said. "I had set out just to…um…have my way with you that night we went to Cesaro's. It had been a game, but something unexpected happened the more I hung around you in the photography studio."

"And what was that?"

"I started to enjoy talking to…or rather spar-ring…with you. There's way more to you than your skimpy blouses and skirts revealed."

"Thank you. About these skimpy outfits, I'm thinking it's probably a good idea to tone them down a bit, at least in the newsroom." Angelica chuckled for the first time since they entered the waiting room. "I do care about projecting a professional image at work."

"So do you think all this clearing the air means we can be friends now?"

"Of course not," she replied without skipping a beat.

"Oh?" Disappointment clouded the gleam in his eyes.

"I was hoping we'd explore other possibilities."

Vince's lips kicked up in his trademark rakish grin and Angelica decided she wouldn't have him any other way. Where was it written that truly nice guys had to be perfect? Who said nice guys couldn't have an edge? Vince Lomax was as edgy as they came, but she now suspected there something more beneath that arrogant, macho, sometimes-a-tad-too-sexist posturing. And she was intrigued enough to find out.

When an emergency room physician with black, choppy bobbed hair and intense onyx eyes appeared, Angelica went to her.

"Hello, I'm Dr. Cho. Which one of you is Carrie-Anne Benton's mother?"

Carrie-Anne?

Angelica and Vince exchanged befuddled glances.

"I am." The pacing woman finally stopped in her tracks. "Is she going to be all right?"

Dr. Cho hesitated when she realized Angelica and Vince were hanging on her words.

"It's all right," the mother assured her. "These are friends of my daughter."

"Carrie-Ann is suffering from a hormonal imbalance and severe dehydration due to her bulimia."

"Bulimia. That can't be. How? When?"

"It's not unusual for parents to be the last to know. If you're not aware of the symptoms, bulimics can easily conceal their condition from those closest to them. A lot of the time their dentists are the first to know."

"Dentists?" the weary-eyed woman echoed.

Vince spoke up. "Yeah, dentists often notice the damage to the teeth caused by stomach acid—from all the purging gradually eroding the enamel in their mouths, right, doc?"

"Correct," Dr. Cho said. "You know someone with bulimia?"

"Knew someone," Vince clarified "She passed away. Heart failure."

"Oh my God!" Ms. Benton shrieked. "My baby isn't going to die, is she?"

"No, we're giving her treatment now. Fluids and such and we'll need to replenish the protein, carbs and potassium deficiency. She should pull through just fine. But she's going to need help, preferably professional counseling. Think you can make sure she gets it? Next time she might not be so lucky."

"Yes, doctor, oh yes! She'll go to counseling even if I have to tie her up and drag her there."

"After this scare, let's hope it won't require all that." Dr. Cho scribbled some notes on her clipboard. "We're going to keep her a few more hours for observation, then we'll release her with some instructions, all right?"

"Yes, doctor. I'll make sure she follows them." Ms. Benton watched the doctor depart, then turned to Angelica and Vince. "I can't thank you enough for making sure Carrie-Anne got to the hospital and for hanging around like you did. Even Carrie-Anne's modeling agent didn't care enough to come check on her. And do you know the wench had the nerve to ask me if Carrie-Anne—or 'Kharisma' as she re-christened herself—fainted before or after the photo shoot? Even after my baby collapsed all that vulture could think about was her damn commission!" The woman became teary-eyed again. "What have I done? What kind of business have I pushed my only child into?"

Angelica rubbed the woman's back to comfort her. "I'm sure…um…Carrie-Anne knows you love her."

Vince tugged a tissue from the box on an end table and passed it to Ms. Benton.

"But I haven't behaved like much of a mother, I've been too busy playing manager, wanting her to be a super model as if my love were contingent on her picture popping up on the cover of some glossy fashion magazine. Since her father died, I've made so many mistakes, I don't know where to begin making it up to her."

"All you can do is start with today, ma'am," Vince said. "Your daughter's going to be fine, which means you have a second chance."

"And I shouldn't waste it on woulda-coulda-shouldas," she said with resolve as she blew into soft pink tissue.

"Right," Angelica replied.

"I'm going to hug my daughter." Ms. Benton moved to the door. "You two coming?"

"You need time alone with Carrie-Anne," Vince said. "Tell her I'll come to your house to see her after work tomorrow."

"No, tell her we'll come to your house after work tomorrow," Angelica added.

"She'll like that," Ms. Benton said, disappearing down the corridor.

"What time is it?" Vince checked his watch. "We've been gone for—"

"Four hours."

Vince suddenly caught Angelica by the waist and pulled her so close she could feel his heart hammering in his strong chest. He covered her mouth with a long, lusty kiss that she eagerly returned.

"Are you in a hurry to get back to the newsroom?" Vince rasped, nibbling at her bottom lip. "Please say no, Angelica."

"No," she moaned as he worked his way down her throat, turning her bones to butter. Neither cared who might be watching.

"So does that mean you'd like to take a nice, long lunch with me at Cesaro's? I promise I won't play with my food."

"Yes, but only on one condition."

"What?"

"You have to call me Angie," she said just before he latched onto her lips again.

CHAPTER 15

After a week passed with no word from Jackson, Savannah concluded that she probably wouldn't hear from him again. He was gone. Just like that, he'd disappeared just as quickly as he'd first appeared.

Since returning from Perryvale, she'd scanned the Silver Spoon dining room looking for his face as she had almost every night since they met. Crushing disappointment followed the realization that another day had passed without him.

After the indignation of how they'd parted wore off, the relentless pain of his rejection set in, followed by the self-flogging. How could she have been so stupid? She'd let down her guard too soon and latched onto his tired old lines out of desperation to believe in the force of romance and true love again.

She looked up and checked the clock on her office wall. Six minutes after seven p.m. As if programmed, she made her rounds amid the tables in the dining room, hoping to see Jackson.

Mr. Watowski caught Savannah by the wrist as she strolled past his table. "Don't worry. He'll come back."

"Excuse me?" she said.

"Your fella, he'll be back, if he has any sense in that thick head of his."

Savannah hadn't recalled ever revealing details about her social life to him. "But—"

"Oh, don't look so surprised. When you've lived as long as this ol' coot has, you learn to listen and watch. I've seen you two together since that first night he showed up here with that brown bag. I saw the sparks flying around you two from the start. And as the days passed I saw the way you two looked at each other."

"And what look was that, Mr. Watowski?" Savannah took the seat across from him. The old man always had a way of making her feel better on the worse days.

He lifted his spoon and dipped into his bowl of mushroom soup. "Looks that told me you were meant for each other, soul mates. You both were so happy and lit up like Christmas trees each time you caught sight of one another."

"I don't know about all that. If he was so crazy for me, where is he now?"

"The most loving, stable couples go through rough patches. Whatever it is, you'll work it out."

How Savannah wanted to grasp onto Mr. Watowski's optimism, but the bottom line was he was merely a sweet old gentleman who didn't know diddly about her relationship with Jackson or what went wrong. In fact, the more she thought about the events leading up to Jackson's abrupt decision to cool things off between the two of them, the more perplexed she became. How could a man who'd declared his love just hours before suddenly become stricken with such a crippling case of commitment-phobia? It just didn't make any sense. It was not as if she'd even said "I love you" first and pressured him to follow up with a declaration of his own. Was he just a jerk who got off making women fall for him, then unceremoniously dumping them only hours after they'd shared their feelings? What she'd like to call her creep-o-meter had been finely tuned since she divorced Bryce. Why hadn't it worked with Jackson?

Another explanation surfaced that she'd immediately brushed off as nonsense. But the more she thought about it, the more plausible it seemed. She'd been curious about that bottle of tablets she'd found in his pocket, but had forgotten all about it once Jackson started hurling accusations about her snooping and lack of trust. And she'd been utterly flummoxed when he'd broken up with her. Could there be a connection between Jackson knowing she'd seen his little sexual booster pills and his angry, irrational outburst? It was too ridiculous! Between the two of them Jackson had seemed so cool, levelheaded and rational. She'd been the one more likely to explode and go off on an overly emotional tear.

Savannah stood and shook her head, determined to push Jackson out of her mind and get back to work. She gave one of her favorite customers her full attention again. "Can I get you something else?"

"You sure can."

"More tea? More crackers? Another helping of soup?"

"An invitation to your wedding when you and that tall fella get hitched."

Savannah patted the old man's shoulder, though her heart ached with the thought of how unlikely that seemed now. "Mr. Watowski, what am I going to do with you?"

❧

"Let me get this straight. You broke things off with the woman of your dreams after a romantic weekend at Grand Gables?" Julian asked over a dizzying array of certified prime beef—porterhouse, New York strip, chateaubriand, and filet mignon at Ryland's, a new high-end steak house on the riverfront.

Jackson had barely managed to get through his week. After a physical exam and a series of tests, the good news from his urologist should have lifted his mood. There had been no permanent damage as a result of those blasted Rocket pills. But he missed Savannah something fierce. Whenever he thought he would succumb to the longing that had rendered him damn near useless at work all week, his pride kicked in. And the humiliation of what had happened to him in Perryvale strengthened his resolve. He was just too weak to face Savannah and acknowledging his fear made him feel like less of a man.

"I didn't invite you here to interrogate me about Savannah." Jackson discreetly jotted notes in the small notebook on his lap. "The only grilling I'm interested in is the kind they do to these steaks here. I need a helper, whose taste buds are as discriminating as mine with beef. Besides, I've told you all you need to know."

Their waiter reappeared.

"I'll have another cognac," Jackson said, though he knew alcohol would have an adverse affect on his ability to do a good job. He'd always made a point to have no more than a few sips of wine when he was gathering column fodder.

Julian waited for their server to disappear before he continued. "But something's still not adding up. I know you were crazy about that woman. You say you two had a big blow-up because you couldn't take her doubt and mistrust anymore."

"Correct."

"What did she do or say exactly that turned you off so completely?" Julian asked as he cut into a tender filet mignon. "If you took her to Grand Gables, I'm assuming you didn't take my advice about waiting before you…um…took things up a few notches. What happened?"

If his brother kept this up, he'd plunge right through the smoke screen Jackson had used to conceal the truth.

"I don't want to discuss this."

"But you don't look happy or relieved at all to be rid of her. So you must still care. You sure there's no hope?"

The waiter arrived with Jackson's drink in the nick of time. Jackson slugged it down so quickly he experienced an immediate buzz. When he ordered another one, he made a decision to scratch work for the night and chalk this up as a personal dinner out on the town with his brother. He'd return to Ryland's at a later date, when he'd cleared his brain enough to actually work.

The waiter reappeared with his second drink.

"C'mon, man. You know I'm your bro. I'm here for you. You can talk to me about anything."

"Not this, my man, not this," Jackson replied just before he drained the glass.

The next morning when Jackson awakened he felt as if his head had been replaced by a cement block.

He slowly swung his legs to the side of the bed and stumbled to the bathroom to retch.

With bleary eyes, he looked in the mirror over the sink, which confirmed that he indeed looked as lousy as he felt. He had to pull himself together in an hour and get to work, but all he wanted to do was crawl between the covers and shut out the world.

He had splashed water over his face and reached for his toothbrush when his phone rang, way too loudly for his pounding head.

He answered on the fifth ring.

"Hey, man." The too-chipper voice of his twin flowed from the other end of the line. "I just wanted to see how you're doing. You were totally wasted when I dropped you off last night. Just wanted to make sure you didn't do something stupid."

"Like what?"

"Before I finally got you to your bed—where you promptly passed out snoring—you were talking about doing a tightrope-like balancing act on the second-floor banister. I haven't seen you that blasted since college. Man, I know it must have been tough on the ol' ego, but you can't let what happened at Grand Gables mess up a good thing. I guarantee it'll be one of those stories you two will laugh about together some day."

What was Julian yammering about? Jackson feigned ignorance until he could figure out how much his brother knew. "What will be one of those stories me and who will laugh about one day?"

"You and Savannah of course. And what happened with the Rocket Booster-pushing cross-dresser in the neon green jumpsuit." Julian chuckled. "Sounds like a story for one of those crazy supermarket tabloids— My Drug Pusher-Man Dresses Like A Wo-Man." Julian stomped on Jackson's last nerve when he began singing the chorus from that old Aerosmith song, "Dude (Looks Like a Lady)" off-key.

"I have no idea what you're talking about," Jackson lied.

"Oh c'mon, don't even try to play dumb. You were too drunk to get that creative and make up a story

complete with details like that. You're trying to say
you forgot what you told me last night?"

"Look, I have one helluva hangover. I haven't
showered or dressed and I have to be at work in an
hour, so goodbye."

"Whoa! Hold on a minute!"

"Talk to you later, Julian. Goodbye."

Julian was still hurling questions just before
Jackson hit the phone's off button.

Jackson considered calling in sick, but he was
already behind schedule. The shower and the pot of
black coffee hadn't done much to clear the thick fog
in his head. He'd locked the front door of the house
and was almost at his car when Julian pulled his blue
Mountaineer behind Jackson's Acura, blocking him
in. Julian, who had obviously just rolled out of bed
himself, vaulted out of his SUV.

"What are you doing here?" Jackson's annoyance
flared again. "I told you I'm on my way to work and
I'm late."

"Well, you're not going to make it there at all if
you don't take a few minutes to talk to me."

"Look, man, I really don't have time for your
games. I'm not self-employed like you so I don't have
the luxury of making my own hours. Now if you'll
just move your ride I'll be on my way."

"Just give me fifteen minutes," Julian pleaded with
outstretched hands.

Jackson wouldn't budge.

"Ten…five minutes."

There was a note of desperation in his twin's voice to which Jackson finally responded. "All right, but make this quick. I've got to go."

Jackson turned and went back inside his house with his brother on his heels.

"You don't look so hot." Julian took a seat in the living room.

"Tell me something I don't know."

"That's exactly what I intend to do, but first I have to apologize for making a joke out of what you revealed to me last night when you were…um…under the influence. About that Rocket Booster stuff you purchased and that side effect that forced you to the emergency room, I'm really sorry that happened to you. But you're fine now, physically, right?"

"Yeah, so?" Jackson couldn't look his brother in the eyes, so he began rifling through the junk mail he scooped off the coffee table.

"And it's just eating you alive that your lady found out you bought a bottle of something like that, am I right? That's what all this anger is about, isn't it? And that's why you're trying to run away from Savannah. Not only did you have to endure those needles in the emergency room, but Savannah finding those tablets on you… It was all way too much. You can't turn back time and tell that…what was that store owner's name again?"

"Trella," Jackson offered with some reluctance.

"You can't tell Trella where to shove those pills. The only thing left in your power is pushing Savannah away, and I don't have to tell you how much you're going to regret that if you don't try to patch things up with her soon."

Jackson sat on the sofa and dropped his head in his hands. "You just don't understand what I've been through these last few months. Feeling like a shell of myself. The worrying and the wondering if I'd ever, you know, be the same again and be able to please a woman. I know there's more to me and a relationship than sex, but still… You and I both know that's an important part. You have no idea what that can do to a man's psyche."

"Oh, but I do, bro. I do."

"What are you saying?"

"I'm saying my situation isn't identical to yours, but I recall having the same doubts, fears and performance anxieties at one time."

"This is the first I'm hearing about this."

"I know. And outside of Darlene and our marriage counselor, I didn't expect anyone to find out." Julian paused, taking a deep breath before continuing. "It was back when Darlene was pregnant with Sasha. From the time I found out she was expecting, it was as if something inside of me froze. I couldn't get aroused enough to have sex with my own wife. What was supposed to be a happy time for both of us really strained our relationship to the point where we even slept in separate beds for about eight months."

"You never said a word." Jackson's jaw dropped.

"Of course, not. I was too ashamed."

"What was the problem?"

"Well, I'll tell you, it wasn't what Darlene thought. She assumed that I thought she was so fat and unattractive that I was totally turned off on her. That wasn't it at all, but she wasn't convinced. And nothing I could say could make her think differently. When she wasn't puking up her guts with morning sickness, she was crying because she thought her husband didn't want her anymore. It was a mess, a real mess, man. And I was whacked out in the head about it. I couldn't talk to anyone, not even you. But now I wish I had. I think you would've helped me put some things in perspective."

"So if it wasn't Darlene's expanding waistline that cooled your ardor, what was it? How did you guys get things back on track in the bedroom? They are back on track, right? You two seem so happy."

"I had this thing, all these hang-ups about the baby being inside of her. And even though her doctor told us sex was fine, I couldn't get it out of my head that I was like this battering ram that would jolt that little bun right out of Darlene's oven. That irrational fear practically crippled me and there was no nookie in my house for months and months. No matter how much I willed myself to perform, I just couldn't get into it. It was awful...for the both of us."

Jackson's lips curved into a smile as he reached over and rubbed his brother's back. "Damn bro, even I know better than that. Sounds as if you grossly over-estimated the…um…power of your…manly assets."

"It's always easier to see the error of someone's else's thinking. Just like I can see you're making a mistake pushing Savannah away. I know she made you happy, but now you're letting your damn ego ruin everything."

"So you and Darlene moved passed the sex famine and things are fine?"

"Yeah, but we had to go to counseling after Sasha was born to repair the holes I'd torn in my relationship with my wife. We'd discussed having more kids, but after the way I'd reacted for those eight months, Darlene was afraid to get pregnant again."

"But you're fine now."

"Yes. I think. I hope. Only time will tell, however. We're feeling strong enough to try again."

Jackson slapped his brother's back, then pulled him closer for a hug. "That's great news! Sasha's going to love having a little brother or sister—"

"To boss around," Julian added as he pushed to his feet and fished his keys out of his pocket. "I guess I'd better let you get going. I hope I've given you something to think about. The type of challenges you and I have encountered are all a part of life, man. You simply hurdle over them and run on."

CHAPTER 16

The Silver Spoon was having one of its busiest days since it opened. The office manager of a local graphic arts business had reserved half the dining room to treat a departing artist to a going-away dinner.

Savannah should've been ecstatic, but thoughts of Jackson's rejection still plagued her. The night before she'd driven over to his place and parked out front. The plan had been to declare her love for him again and insist that he talk to her and tell her why he'd jerked away just when emotions deepened. Was it really commitment-phobia or was his need to get away tied to that bottle of tablets she'd discovered in his pants? She was going to demand answers! An explanation.

Then, based upon how forthcoming he was, she was going to launch herself into his arms and assure him that nothing mattered but the two of them staying together. That had been the plan until she came to her senses. She refused to go crawling after him when she had done nothing wrong. She ended up simply watching his house because she couldn't bring herself to get out of the car and knock on the door.

She drove away in tears. Her pride might have remained intact, but her heart was still in shambles.

She plastered on a smile as she threaded her way through the tables of diners. That part of her that still wanted to believe Mr. Watowski stole glances at the door every time someone entered. To spare herself the torture, she slipped back to her office.

She'd just taken her seat when Troy poked his head inside. "Savannah. You're not going to believe who's here."

"Jackson?" she asked, hopefully.

"No, sorry. It's a Mr. Gavin Baker, says he's an…um…sanitarian from the health department."

"The health department? Oh, he's going to do one of those surprise inspections I've heard about," Savannah said casually.

"I thought you'd be more nervous."

"Why? We have nothing to worry about. Just inform the staff and make sure it's business as usual," she replied. Savannah busied herself in her office while Mr. Baker did his job.

Less than an hour later Troy came to fetch her. "Savannah, we have a big problem."

"What?" She popped up from her chair.

Before Troy could reply, Mr. Baker had squeezed by him and presented Savannah with pages from his clipboard.

Savannah scanned the paper. "What's this?"

"I found numerous critical violations on the premises," Mr. Baker said as he scribbled more notes.

"Many of which could be a major contributing factor to food-borne illnesses."

"Oh my gosh!" she shrieked.

"Among them, what appeared to be mouse droppings in the pantry where dry food goods are stored. Also, with my thermometer I found food not being stored at appropriate temperatures."

"What?" Savannah's jaw dropped. "That can't be! There must be some mistake."

"No mistake. If you'll just step out here, I can show you," the man said.

Savannah did as instructed.

"Is everything all right?" Eloise asked as she continued her supervising duties with Percy and Emma Jean.

"You go on and continue working." Savannah tried tossing them a reassuring smile. "Everything is going to be fine."

Inside the pantry the floor was covered with tiny bits of something that looked like black rice. She swore that hadn't been there when she opened the restaurant that morning. "Where did all these come from?"

"Mice, I believe. Looks as if they turned your walk-in pantry into a veritable litter box," Mr. Baker said smartly as he continued making notes on his clipboard. "I don't believe I've ever seen a case this bad. And if you'll step over here, I'll show you a silverware drawer full of what appears to be dead fruit flies."

"What!" Savannah's hands flew to her temples where a migraine flared. If she hadn't reached out to brace herself against the doorjamb, she probably would have collapsed. "This can't be happening."

"Don't worry, sis. I'll have that stuff cleaned right up," Troy said. "As long as we take care of the violations before you leave, everything should be fine, right?"

"Yes, to avoid closure of this establishment all critical violations must be corrected by the operator while I'm on the premises," the man confirmed.

"I don't know how those nasty things got there, but I can assure you we are going to clean up and I'm going to get to the bottom of this," Savannah vowed, anger bubbling inside of her.

"Before you begin your investigation you'd better call a good repairman to fix your refrigerators. It looks as if both of them are on the fritz, which is why your food is not stored at appropriate temperatures. I'm afraid if that's not fixed before I leave I'm going to have to insist that you close until it's taken care of."

Savannah frantically worked down a Yellow Pages list of repair services, but no one had anyone available immediately.

Mr. Baker passed Savannah an additional notice. "I'm sorry, but I can't allow you to remain open under the circumstances. The public's health is at risk. You'll have to clear the place immediately."

"But…" Savannah pleaded in a thin voice.

"I'm sorry. I have no choice," the man said.

Troy went to her and wrapped her in a hug. "I'll take care of it, sis. You go back to your office."

Savannah was too stunned and emotionally drained to argue. Woodenly, she walked to her office and closed the door. Once in her chair, she slumped over her desk and wept.

Savannah remained at her desk long after her staff left. She convinced Troy to leave, only because she'd pleaded that she needed this time alone.

She ambled through her restaurant as an eerie quiet settled over the place. How could everything so right in her life have gone so wrong? First Jackson, now the Silver Spoon.

A storm broke as she dropped on a table near the restaurant's front. Lightning streaked across the sky and rain splattered the picture window. More tears came down as hard as the rain, until she heard pounding at the back door.

She quickly dried her eyes to look through the peephole. On the other side she saw a drenched Clara.

Savannah opened the door, quickly ushering the woman inside. "Clara, what are you doing out in weather like this? You guys had the rest of the night off."

"I know," the woman said through chattering teeth. "But I had to come to see how you were doing. You looked so sad when Troy sent us home."

"Let me make you some tea, you're shivering."

"I'll be fine." She rubbed her bony arms to generate warmth.

"How did you get over here? Does the bus run this time of night?" Savannah heated some water in the microwave and reached for packets of Earl Grey on the counter.

"No, I walked back here."

"But why? If you simply wanted to check on me you could've phoned."

"I needed to talk to you, face to face."

"Is something wrong? It's not Mikey, is it? He's doing better, right?"

"See, that's why I had to come over here tonight— even if it meant swimming here. You've got your own problems and you're still worrying about someone else."

"Let's go talk in the dining room."

Savannah returned to her chair near the front window and Clara sat across from her.

"What did you need to talk about?" Savannah asked.

"About what happened today with the inspection."

"Go on."

Tears welled up in the woman's eyes.

"Don't worry, Clara, we won't be closed for long. A day or two max, I swear it. So you don't have to worry about your job."

"It's not that." The woman began to cry in earnest and Savannah tugged a napkin out of a holder and passed it to her. "I have a job here now, but I'm sure I won't once you hear what I have to say."

Savannah's braced herself for more bad news. "What is it, Clara?"

"I—I…" Clara looked down at her hands, sucked in a deep breath and started again. "I scattered all those mouse droppings in the walk-in pantries and the dead flies in the silverware drawer. And I disabled both of the refrigerators."

Savannah flinched at the stab of betrayal. "But Clara, why? Why would you do such awful things?"

"Savannah, I'm so sorry," she wailed. "I saw how much that suspension hurt you. I felt so low—especially after everything you've done for me. Nothing and no one should've made me do something so sneaky and underhanded. You've been nothing but kind to me."

"Someone put you up to this?"

Clara nodded slowly.

"Who?" Savannah slapped her hand against own forehead. "Wait. I don't even know why I'm bothering to ask. Bryce made you do those things, right?"

"Yes."

"Why that miserable…" Savannah's words dissolved when she pounded the table with her fist. "Why can't he just leave me the hell alone and let me move on with my life?"

"Remember that day when you left for your weekend away with your boyfriend, that food critic?"

Savannah tried to ignore the dull ache inside that immediately surfaced when she thought of her last day with Jackson. "Go on."

"You were going to let me leave early to go home to take care of Mikey."

"Yeah, your mother-in-law was ill and couldn't care for him."

"I was waiting at the bus stop to catch the 456 Crestmont to go home when Mr. Martin pulled up in his big fancy car and offered me a ride. Normally I wouldn't accept a ride from a stranger, but I'd seen you two talking and you were smiling when the two of you left your office that day. And he was so well dressed. He looked rich. I figured it was okay."

Savannah recalled how happy she'd been that day. That smile had had nothing to do with Bryce and everything to do with Jackson.

"During the drive he was so nice, chatting and asking me all kinds of questions about the Silver Spoon and how I liked working here. I told him how great you were and how you'd given me a job here when I desperately needed one. I made the mistake of telling him about my little Mikey. By the time we made it to my place, he'd used that info to suck me in. He promised me enough money to pay the balance of Mikey's medical bills and still have a big chunk left over for future medical expenses."

"And in return all you had to do was sabotage my restaurant."

"Yes, it was as if he forced me to choose between something to help my child and my loyalty to you."

"That rat!" Savannah ground out.

"But I agreed to help him and now look what's happened."

"I don't blame you, Clara, I understand your dilemma. You have a sick child to think about. Though I do wish you'd come to me with this sooner, I'm just glad you saw fit to tell me what my no-good, scum-sucking ex-husband has been up to." She thought for a moment. "How did Bryce know that health department inspector was coming?"

"I asked him about that. He paid several people to file complaints on this place and I guess he has connections who can make things happen when he needs them to. He told me not to worry about anything except doing my part when I got his signal via a pager he gave me. A few days before he had some guy demonstrate how to easily disable the two refrigerators just before the inspector arrived."

Of course, more of those dreaded connections of his. Bryce had them everywhere. That *Tribune* honcho that Jackson had told her about rushed to mind.

"Again, I'm so sorry, Savannah, but I just couldn't live with myself if I didn't tell you. When Mr. Martin finds out I told you he was involved, he'll probably cancel that check he gave me for Mikey. I'm going to tell him I don't want any money I had to earn like this, anyway."

Savannah reached for the woman's hand. "No, don't! Don't tell him you told me anything! And I insist that you take his money for Mikey. Some of his money should be used to help those who really need it."

"But—"

"Knowing something good will come out of my restaurant's temporary closing makes me feel a little better and it certainly puts things into perspective. I was sitting here just wallowing in self-pity and when I think of what you've had to endure with your little boy…" Her voice caught. "Anyway, it just warms my heart to see how much you love him."

"So you're not angry at me?"

"No. Bryce used you and your love for your son to attack me."

"I know you say you're not blaming me, but I can't imagine you'll still want me working here…I mean, after everything."

"You're wrong. I expect you to show up to work just like everyone else after the mess has been straightened out."

Clara's eyes welled up again, just as Troy emerged through the swinging door.

"I thought I sent you home for the night," Savannah said to Troy.

"I couldn't go to sleep until I came back to check on you, sis. What are you doing here, Clara?"

"Nobody has to know about our little talk," Savannah whispered to Clara. "Troy and the others might not understand."

Clara stood. "I was worried about Savannah, too. I came back to check on her. I was just leaving, though."

"In this rain? The buses have stopped running." Troy shook rain off his umbrella.

"Troy, would you be a sweetheart and give Clara a lift? Her place is on your route home."

"Sure, no problem. Are you about ready to leave, too?"

"Yeah," Savannah replied. "You two go ahead. I've got to tidy up my office a bit. I'll be right behind you."

"Promise?" Troy gave his sister a farewell hug.

"Promise." Savannah stepped away from Troy.

Clara moved to embrace her as she whispered in her ear. "Thank you for everything. And I promise I won't ever let you down again."

Troy and Clara darted to the Taurus parked near the exit.

Savannah stood in the doorway, loving the feel of the cool rain pelting her skin. She watched until the taillights of her brother's car disappeared.

She'd turned to go back inside when she heard something. Was it the wind or someone calling out to her?

"Savannah!"

Through the rain she managed to make out the tall male raincoat-clad form sprinting toward her. As he neared the door he dropped his hood.

Jackson!

"Savannah, we need to talk." He stood just outside the threshold, awaiting her invitation inside.

Her heart hammered in her chest. He looked so handsome. It was all she could do to keep from tackling the man.

"I heard what happened today," he said, peeling out of his wet coat.

"But how?"

"A colleague's wife was at that group celebrating at your restaurant today. She told him the gathering had been cut short and why. And of course, he told me."

Savannah tried to keep disappointment out of her voice. She had hoped Jackson had come because he realized that he'd made a mistake by walking away from what they had. But this wasn't about his feelings for her, but his interest in the success of her restaurant, which he obviously still viewed as a reflection on him. After all, he'd invested not only ideas, but time. He'd found the challenge of it intoxicating. It wasn't just something he could wash his hands of as easily as he'd done with her.

"You must be devastated," he said. "I know how hard you worked on this place and to have something like this happen just when things were really starting to take off…"

"We'll survive," she said tightly. "I'll bounce back like I always do."

"Yes, you will."

"Then why are you here?"

"I guess I thought I needed an excuse to see you—especially after the way things ended in Perryvale."

"Oh?" Her heart leapt, but she didn't want to appear too eager to pounce on any half-ass apology he tossed at her.

"The bottom line is I behaved like a first-class jerk who simply couldn't get over himself. And I'm hoping it's not too late for you to consider giving me a second chance. I want to make it up to you. My rant that day had absolutely nothing to do with you. It was about a demon I'd been fighting for months before we met."

"Something to do with that bottle of tablets I inadvertently found in your pocket?"

Jackson took the next half hour to explain his surgery and the psychological effect it had had on him. And how his insecurities had led him to do something stupid like pop that supplement without consulting his doctor first.

If only he'd been open about his concerns before they'd made love, he could've saved himself so much grief and the pain of that emergency room visit, Savannah thought. But she knew it was a guy thing. Males could get really weirded out about anything they believed could stamp a big question mark on their manhood or virility.

Jackson drew her into his arms. "Oh, lady, you don't know how much I've missed holding you like this. And now that I have you in my arms again, I'm never letting go."

"So does this sorta-kinda mean you still love me?" She gazed up into his eyes.

"Absolutely positively, and you?"

"Ditto."

Jackson swept her off her feet and she wrapped her legs around his long, muscular torso. He dropped kisses all over her face and tugged up her skirt and slid his hands inside her panties as he moved across the dining room floor.

"Hey, where are you are taking me?" she asked between breathless kisses.

"To the moon, of course. And no Rocket Booster is required."

EPILOGUE

Three weeks later…

"I'm so glad you called," Bryce said as Savannah shoved the last bite of devil's food cake inside his mouth. "This is just like old times. A romantic picnic in my office. Everything was so delicious."

Savannah smiled sweetly.

He patted his belly. "All full," he teased with a satisfied grin.

"You sure you're not going to go for a third slice of the cake?" Savannah asked as she packed up the plates and silverware from their picnic lunch and placed them back inside her wicker basket. "You know, Bryce, I thought about what you said a few weeks ago…about us reconciling, I mean."

"So I take it this little surprise picnic is a new beginning for us?"

"Yeah, sort of." She rolled up the blanket she had spread across his office floor and jammed it inside her basket. "It's well…actually…the beginning of the end, you bozo."

"Bozo?" Bryce sputtered, scrambling to his feet. "But I don't understand. I thought we were… What about us getting back together?"

"Is that what you thought?" Savannah threw her head back and chuckled. "Now I wonder where you got a stupid idea like that."

"The picnic! The wine! You feeding me cake!"

"Just wanted you to get one last sampling of what you'll never, ever have again. And I wanted you to be one of the first to hear the news from me. Drum roll, please! I'm engaged!"

"To that food critic?"

"Who else?" Savannah confirmed gleefully, then scooped up her basket. She walked to the door and flung it open dramatically. "And if you ever bother me again, my future husband and I will not hesitate to hire a lawyer and have you sued for harassment. Buh-byyyye!"

Bryce, stunned silent for once, watched Savannah march to her car, where Jackson awaited her.

She shoved the diamond Jackson had given her back on and playfully rippled her fingers at Bryce before climbing inside.

"Everything go as planned, sweetheart?" Jackson gave her a quick kiss on the lips, then started the engine.

"Uh-huh. Like clockwork." Savannah hadn't wanted to stoop to Bryce's level but he'd pulled so many capers on her, he had it coming. She'd recently discovered that he was also the one behind the flasher, the busted pipes, the cockroaches in those bargain bags of flour and Felix's resignation.

It was only fair that she sought a little bit of retribution for all the trouble he'd caused her.

"You're not having second thoughts about sticking it to Bryce, are you?" Jackson asked as she secured her seat belt.

"Oh no. You know what they say about how revenge is best served cold. Well, it's even better when it comes as one of Eloise's sinful desserts."

Besides Savannah's love for Jackson, one thing was for certain. She wouldn't have to worry about Bryce bothering her for the next few hours. He would be way too busy once that laxative-laced cake he'd just wolfed down worked its way through his system.

"That's my girl." Jackson smiled, then dropped another kiss on her lips

"You got that right. I am your girl. Always and forever."

2009 Reprint Mass Market Titles

January

I'm Gonna Make You Love Me
Gwyneth Bolton
ISBN-13: 978-1-58571-291-5
ISBN-10: 1-58571-291-4
$6.99

Shades of Desire
Monica White
ISBN-13: 978-1-58571-292-2
ISBN-10: 1-58571-292-2
$6.99

February

A Love of Her Own
Cheris Hodges
ISBN-13: 978-1-58571-293-9
ISBN-10: 1-58571-293-0
$6.99

Color of Trouble
Dyanne Davis
ISBN-13: 978-1-58571-294-6
ISBN-10: 1-58571-096-6
$6.99

March

Twist of Fate
Beverly Clark
ISBN-13: 978-1-58571-295-3
ISBN-10: 1-58571-295-7
$6.99

Chances
Pamela Leigh Starr
ISBN-13: 978-1-58571-296-0
ISBN-10: 1-58571-296-5
$6.99

April

Sinful Intentions
Crystal Rhodes
ISBN-13: 978-1-585712-297-7
ISBN-10: 1-58571-297-3
$6.99

Rock Star
Roslyn Hardy Holcomb
ISBN-13: 978-1-58571-298-4
$6.99

May

Path of Fire
T.T. Henderson
ISBN-13: 978-1-58571-343-1
ISBN-10: 1-58571-343-0
$6.99

Caught Up in the Rapture
Lisa Riley
ISBN-13: 978-1-58571-344-8
ISBN-10: 1-58571-344-9
$6.99

June

Reckless Surrender
Rochelle Alers
ISBN-13: 978-1-58571-345-5
ISBN-10: 1-58571-345-7
$6.99

No Ordinary Love
Angela Weaver
ISBN-13: 978-1-58571-346-2
ISBN-10: 1-58571-346-5
$6.99

2009 Reprint Mass Market Titles (continued)

July

Intentional Mistakes
Michele Sudler
ISBN-13: 978-1-58571-347-9
ISBN-10: 1-58571-347-3
$6.99

It's in His Kiss
Reon Laudat
ISBN-13: 978-1-58571-348-6
ISBN-10: 1-58571-348-1
$6.99

August

Unfinished Love Affair
Barbara Keaton
ISBN-13: 978-1-58571-349-3
ISBN-10: 1-58571-349-X
$6.99

A Perfect Place to Pray
I.L Goodwin
ISBN-13: 978-1-58571-299-1
ISBN-10: 1-58571-299-X
$6.99

September

Love in High Gear
Charlotte Roy
ISBN-13: 978-1-58571-355-4
ISBN-10: 1-58571-355-4
$6.99

Ebony Eyes
Kei Swanson
ISBN-13: 978-1-58571-356-1
ISBN-10: 1-58571-356-2
$6.99

October

Midnight Clear, Part I
Leslie Esdale/Carmen Green
ISBN-13: 978-1-58571-357-8
ISBN-10: 1-58571-357-0
$6.99

Midnight Clear, Part II
Gwynne Forster/Monica
    Jackson
ISBN-13: 978-1-58571-358-5
ISBN-10: 1-58571-358-9
$6.99

November

Midnight Peril
Vicki Andrews
ISBN-13: 978-1-58571-359-2
ISBN-10: 1-58571-359-7
$6.99

One Day at a Time
Bella McFarland
ISBN-13: 978-1-58571-360-8
ISBN-10: 1-58571-360-0
$6.99

December

Just an Affair
Eugenia O'Neal
ISBN-13: 978-1-58571-361-5
ISBN-10: 1-58571-361-9
$6.99

Shades of Brown
Denise Becker
ISBN-13: 978-1-58571-362-2
ISBN-10: 1-58571-362-7
$6.99

2009 New Mass Market Titles

January

Singing A Song...
Crystal Rhodes
ISBN-13: 978-1-58571-283-0
$6.99

Look Both Ways
Joan Early
ISBN-13: 978-1-58571-284-7
$6.99

February

Six O'Clock
Katrina Spencer
ISBN-13: 978-1-58571-285-4
$6.99

Red Sky
Renee Alexis
ISBN-13: 978-1-58571-286-1
$6.99

March

Anything But Love
Celya Bowers
ISBN-13: 978-1-58571-287-8
$6.99

Tempting Faith
Crystal Hubbard
ISBN-13: 978-1-58571-288-5
$6.99

April

If I Were Your Woman
LaConnie Taylor-Jones
ISBN-13: 978-1-58571-289-2
$6.99

Best of Luck Elsewhere
Trisha Haddad
ISBN-13: 978-1-58571-290-8
$6.99

May

All I'll Ever Need
Mildred Riley
ISBN-13: 978-1-58571-335-6
$6.99

A Place Like Home
Alicia Wiggins
ISBN-13: 978-1-58571-336-3
$6.99

June

Best Foot Forward
Michele Sudler
ISBN-13: 978-1-58571-337-0
$6.99

It's in the Rhythm
Sammie Ward
ISBN-13: 978-1-58571-338-7
$6.99

2009 New Mass Market Titles (continued)

July

Checks and Balances
Elaine Sims
ISBN-13: 978-1-58571-339-4
$6.99

Save Me
Africa Fine
ISBN-13: 978-1-58571-340-0
$6.99

August

When Lightening Strikes
Michele Cameron
ISBN-13: 978-1-58571-369-1
$6.99

Blindsided
Tammy Williams
ISBN-13: 978-1-58571-342-4
$6.99

September

2 Good
Celya Bowers
ISBN-13: 978-1-58571-350-9
$6.99

Waiting for Mr. Darcy
Chamein Canton
ISBN-13: 978-1-58571-351-6
$6.99

October

Fireflies
Joan Early
ISBN-13: 978-1-58571-352-3
$6.99

Frost On My Window
Angela Weaver
ISBN-13: 978-1-58571-353-0
$6.99

November

Waiting in the Shadows
Michele Sudler
ISBN-13: 978-1-58571-364-6
$6.99

Fixin' Tyrone
Keith Walker
ISBN-13: 978-1-58571-365-3
$6.99

December

Dream Keeper
Gail McFarland
ISBN-13: 978-1-58571-366-0
$6.99

Another Memory
Pamela Ridley
ISBN-13: 978-1-58571-367-7
$6.99

Other Genesis Press, Inc. Titles

A Dangerous Deception	J.M. Jeffries	$8.95
A Dangerous Love	J.M. Jeffries	$8.95
A Dangerous Obsession	J.M. Jeffries	$8.95
A Drummer's Beat to Mend	Kei Swanson	$9.95
A Happy Life	Charlotte Harris	$9.95
A Heart's Awakening	Veronica Parker	$9.95
A Lark on the Wing	Phyliss Hamilton	$9.95
A Love of Her Own	Cheris F. Hodges	$9.95
A Love to Cherish	Beverly Clark	$8.95
A Risk of Rain	Dar Tomlinson	$8.95
A Taste of Temptation	Reneé Alexis	$9.95
A Twist of Fate	Beverly Clark	$8.95
A Voice Behind Thunder	Carrie Elizabeth Greene	$6.99
A Will to Love	Angie Daniels	$9.95
Acquisitions	Kimberley White	$8.95
Across	Carol Payne	$12.95
After the Vows	Leslie Esdaile	$10.95
(Summer Anthology)	T.T. Henderson	
	Jacqueline Thomas	
Again, My Love	Kayla Perrin	$10.95
Against the Wind	Gwynne Forster	$8.95
All I Ask	Barbara Keaton	$8.95
Always You	Crystal Hubbard	$6.99
Ambrosia	T.T. Henderson	$8.95
An Unfinished Love Affair	Barbara Keaton	$8.95
And Then Came You	Dorothy Elizabeth Love	$8.95
Angel's Paradise	Janice Angelique	$9.95
At Last	Lisa G. Riley	$8.95
Best of Friends	Natalie Dunbar	$8.95
Beyond the Rapture	Beverly Clark	$9.95
Blame It on Paradise	Crystal Hubbard	$6.99
Blaze	Barbara Keaton	$9.95
Bliss, Inc.	Chamein Canton	$6.99
Blood Lust	J.M.Jeffries	$9.95
Blood Seduction	J.M. Jeffries	$9.95
Bodyguard	Andrea Jackson	$9.95
Boss of Me	Diana Nyad	$8.95
Bound by Love	Beverly Clark	$8.95
Breeze	Robin Hampton Allen	$10.95

Other Genesis Press, Inc. Titles (continued)

Other Genesis Press, Inc. Titles (continued)

Everything But Love	Natalie Dunbar	$8.95
Falling	Natalie Dunbar	$9.95
Fate	Pamela Leigh Starr	$8.95
Finding Isabella	A.J. Garrotto	$8.95
Forbidden Quest	Dar Tomlinson	$10.95
Forever Love	Wanda Y. Thomas	$8.95
From the Ashes	Kathleen Suzanne	$8.95
	Jeanne Sumerix	
Gentle Yearning	Rochelle Alers	$10.95
Glory of Love	Sinclair LeBeau	$10.95
Go Gentle Into That	Malcom Boyd	$12.95
Good Night		
Goldengroove	Mary Beth Craft	$16.95
Groove, Bang, and Jive	Steve Cannon	$8.99
Hand in Glove	Andrea Jackson	$9.95
Hard to Love	Kimberley White	$9.95
Hart & Soul	Angie Daniels	$8.95
Heart of the Phoenix	A.C. Arthur	$9.95
Heartbeat	Stephanie Bedwell-Grime	$8.95
Hearts Remember	M. Loui Quezada	$8.95
Hidden Memories	Robin Allen	$10.95
Higher Ground	Leah Latimer	$19.95
Hitler, the War, and the Pope	Ronald Rychiak	$26.95
How to Write a Romance	Kathryn Falk	$18.95
I Married a Reclining Chair	Lisa M. Fuhs	$8.95
I'll Be Your Shelter	Giselle Carmichael	$8.95
I'll Paint a Sun	A.J. Garrotto	$9.95
Icie	Pamela Leigh Starr	$8.95
Illusions	Pamela Leigh Starr	$8.95
Indigo After Dark Vol. I	Nia Dixon/Angelique	$10.95
Indigo After Dark Vol. II	Dolores Bundy/	$10.95
	Cole Riley	
Indigo After Dark Vol. III	Montana Blue/	$10.95
	Coco Morena	
Indigo After Dark Vol. IV	Cassandra Colt/	$14.95
Indigo After Dark Vol. V	Delilah Dawson	$14.95
Indiscretions	Donna Hill	$8.95
Intentional Mistakes	Michele Sudler	$9.95
Interlude	Donna Hill	$8.95

Other Genesis Press, Inc. Titles (continued)

Other Genesis Press, Inc. Titles (continued)

No Commitment Required	Seressia Glass	$8.95
No Regrets	Mildred E. Riley	$8.95
Not His Type	Chamein Canton	$6.99
Nowhere to Run	Gay G. Gunn	$10.95
O Bed! O Breakfast!	Rob Kuehnle	$14.95
Object of His Desire	A.C. Arthur	$8.95
Office Policy	A.C. Arthur	$9.95
Once in a Blue Moon	Dorianne Cole	$9.95
One Day at a Time	Bella McFarland	$8.95
One of These Days	Michele Sudler	$9.95
Outside Chance	Louisa Dixon	$24.95
Passion	T.T. Henderson	$10.95
Passion's Blood	Cherif Fortin	$22.95
Passion's Furies	AlTonya Washington	$6.99
Passion's Journey	Wanda Y. Thomas	$8.95
Past Promises	Jahmel West	$8.95
Path of Fire	T.T. Henderson	$8.95
Path of Thorns	Annetta P. Lee	$9.95
Peace Be Still	Colette Haywood	$12.95
Picture Perfect	Reon Carter	$8.95
Playing for Keeps	Stephanie Salinas	$8.95
Pride & Joi	Gay G. Gunn	$8.95
Promises Made	Bernice Layton	$6.99
Promises to Keep	Alicia Wiggins	$8.95
Quiet Storm	Donna Hill	$10.95
Reckless Surrender	Rochelle Alers	$6.95
Red Polka Dot in a World Full of Plaid	Varian Johnson	$12.95
Reluctant Captive	Joyce Jackson	$8.95
Rendezvous With Fate	Jeanne Sumerix	$8.95
Revelations	Cheris F. Hodges	$8.95
Rivers of the Soul	Leslie Esdaile	$8.95
Rocky Mountain Romance	Kathleen Suzanne	$8.95
Rooms of the Heart	Donna Hill	$8.95
Rough on Rats and Tough on Cats	Chris Parker	$12.95
Secret Library Vol. 1	Nina Sheridan	$18.95
Secret Library Vol. 2	Cassandra Colt	$8.95
Secret Thunder	Annetta P. Lee	$9.95

Other Genesis Press, Inc. Titles (continued)

Other Genesis Press, Inc. Titles (continued)

GENESIS MOVIE NETWORK

The Indigo Colletion

J U L Y   2 0 0 9

Starring: Sean Connery, Wesley Snipes
When: July 3 - July 19
Time Period: Noon to 2AM

An ex-investigator (Sean Connery) with expert knowledge of Japanese customs is called in to help a detective (Wesley Snipes) solve a prostitute's murder. Committed during the height of a corporate gala, the crime was captured on video -- but the evidence has been suspiciously altered. As they work together to solve the case, the unlikely partners uncover a chain of corporate corruption that's nearly as gruesome as the victim's death.

Allied Media Partners
1629 K St., NW, Suite 300, Washington, DC 20006
202-349-5785

GENESIS MOVIE NETWORK

The Indigo Collection

AUGUST/SEPTEMBER 2009

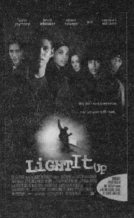

Starring: Usher, Forest Whitaker
When: August 22 - September 6
Time Period: Noon to 2AM

Taps meets The Breakfast Club in the inner city in this late 1990s answer to the Brat Pack flicks of the 1980s (with ex-Brat Packer Judd Nelson in attendance). When an incident with a high school security guard (Forest Whitaker) pushes a decent kid (Usher Raymond) past his breaking point, the boy unites a diverse and troubled student body to take the school hostage until they can make their voices heard.

Allied Media Partners
1629 K St., NW, Suite 300, Washington, DC 20006
202-349-5785

GENESIS MOVIE NETWORK

The Indigo Collection

SEPTEMBER 2009

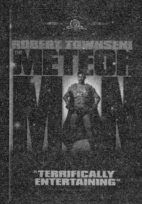

"TERRIFICALLY ENTERTAINING"

Starring: Robert Townsend, Marla Gibbs, Eddie Griffin
When: September 5 - September 20
Time Period: Noon to 2AM

While being chased by neighborhood thugs, weak-kneed high school teacher Jefferson Reed (Robert Townsend) is struck by a meteor and suddenly develops superhuman strength and abilities: He can fly, talk to dogs and absorb knowledge from any book in 30 seconds! His mom creates a costume, and he begins practicing his newfound skills in secret. But his nightly community improvements soon draw the wrath of the bad guys who terrorize his block.

Allied Media Partners
1629 K St., NW, Suite 300, Washington, DC 20006
202-349-5785

Order Form

Mail to: Genesis Press, Inc.
P.O. Box 101
Columbus, MS 39703

Name _____

Address _____

City/State _____ Zip _____

Telephone _____

Ship to (if different from above)

Name _____

Address _____

City/State _____ Zip _____

Telephone _____

Credit Card Information

Credit Card # _____ ☐ Visa ☐ Mastercard

Expiration Date (mm/yy) _____ ☐ AmEx ☐ Discover

Qty.	Author	Title	Price	Total

Use this order form, or call 1-888-INDIGO-1		
Total for books		_____
Shipping and handling: $5 first two books, $1 each additional book		_____
Total S & H		_____
Total amount enclosed		_____

Mississippi residents add 7% sales tax

4410